## Cast of Characters

**Kate Rebel:** Matriarch of the Rebel family.

**Falcon:** The oldest son—the strong one. Reunited with his wife, Leah, and proud father of Eden and John.

**Egan:** The loner. Married to Rachel Hollister, daughter of the man who put him in jail.

**Quincy:** The peacemaker. Married to Jenny Walker, his childhood best friend.

**Elias:** The fighter. Falls in love with the archenemy of the family's daughter.

**Paxton:** The lover. Never met a woman he couldn't have, but the woman he wants doesn't want him.

**Jude:** The serious, responsible one. Back together with his first love, Paige Wheeler, and raising their son, Zane.

**Phoenix:** The wild one and the youngest. He's carefree until Child Protective Services says he's the father of a small boy.

**Abraham (Abe) Rebel:** Paternal grandfather.

**Jericho Johnson:** Egan's friend from prison.

Dear Reader,

This is the fifth book in the Texas Rebels series. If you've read any of the Rebel books, you know they're about seven brothers dealing with life after their father's death in the small town of Horseshoe, Texas.

Phoenix is the youngest and their mother's favorite. He's a carefree, fun-loving guy who doesn't take anything too seriously. Until he finds out he's the father of a two-year-old boy. Then he grows up quickly. To complicate matters, he does the unthinkable: falls in love with Rosemary (Rosie) McCray Wilcott, the daughter of the family's archenemy.

Rosemary has had a difficult life. Her father forced her to marry an abusive man. After she divorces him, the McCray family disowns her. She's a loner and doesn't allow anyone in until Phoenix breaks through her defenses. She wants to love Phoenix and his son, but there's so much standing in their way.

This was an emotional story to write as Phoenix must fight for the woman he loves. He goes against family and everything he was taught. I had my doubts if there was going to be a happy ending for Phoenix and Rosie. But love has a way of working miracles. I love a story about a man who's willing to risk it all for the woman he loves and I hope you will, too.

Until the next Rebel book, with love and thanks,

*Linda*

You can email me at Lw1508@aol.com; send me a message on Facebook.com/lindawarrenauthor or on Twitter, @texauthor; write me at PO Box 5182, Bryan, TX 77805; or visit my website at lindawarren.net. Your mail and thoughts are deeply appreciated.

# TEXAS REBELS: PHOENIX

## LINDA WARREN

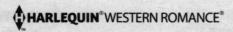

HARLEQUIN® WESTERN ROMANCE®

ISBN-13: 978-0-373-75722-0

Texas Rebels: Phoenix

Copyright © 2016 by Linda Warren

Printed in U.S.A.

A two-time RITA® Award–nominated author, **Linda Warren** has written thirty-eight books for Harlequin and has received the Readers' Choice Award, the Holt Medallion, the Booksellers' Best Award, the Book Buyers Best Award, the Golden Quill and the RT Reviewers' Choice Best Book Award. A native Texan, she is a member of Romance Writers of America and the West Houston chapter. She lives in College Station with her husband and a menagerie of animals, including a Canada goose named Broken Wing. You can learn more about Linda and her books at lindawarren.net.

## Books by Linda Warren

### Harlequin American Romance

*The Cowboy's Return*
*Once a Cowboy*
*Texas Heir*
*The Sheriff of Horseshoe, Texas*
*Her Christmas Hero*
*Tomas: Cowboy Homecoming*
*One Night in Texas*
*A Texas Holiday Miracle*

### *Texas Rebels*

*Texas Rebels: Egan*
*Texas Rebels: Falcon*
*Texas Rebels: Quincy*
*Texas Rebels: Jude*

Visit lindawarren.net for more titles.

To Christi Hendricks—for organizing
sixteen years of book signings.

## Acknowledgments

A special thanks to Vanessa Carmona Hoke
for taking the time to share her knowledge of
the Department of Family and Protective Services.
And to Carrol Abendroth, barrel racer,
for discussing the rodeo and barrel racing.
And to PRCA for all their information.

# Prologue

My name is Kate Rebel. I married John Rebel when I was eighteen years old and then bore him seven sons. We worked the family ranch, which John later inherited. We put everything we had into buying more land so our sons would have a legacy. We didn't have much, but we had love.

The McCray Ranch borders Rebel Ranch on the east and the McCrays have forever been a thorn in my family's side. They've cut our fences, dammed up creeks to limit our water supply and shot one of our prize bulls. Ezra McCray threatened to shoot our sons if he caught them jumping his fences again. We tried to keep our boys away, but they are boys—young and wild.

One day Jude and Phoenix, two of our youngest, were out riding together. When John heard shots, he immediately went to find his boys. They lay on the ground, blood oozing from their heads. Ezra McCray was astride a horse twenty yards away with a rifle in his hand. John drew his gun and fired, killing Ezra instantly. Both boys survived with only minor wounds. Since my husband was protecting his children, he didn't spend even one night in jail. This escalated the feud that still goes on today.

The man I knew as my husband died that day. He

couldn't live with what he'd done and started to drink heavily. I had to take over the ranch and the raising of our boys. John died ten years later. We've all been affected by the tragedy, especially my sons.

They are grown men now and deal in different ways with the pain of losing their father. One day I pray my boys will be able to put this behind them and live healthy, normal lives with women who will love them the way I loved their father.

# Chapter One

*Phoenix: the youngest son—the fun-loving one.*

*The cowboy's last ride.*

Phoenix Rebel had been called a lot of things, but he'd never been called daddy. Yet the lady sitting on his mother's leather sectional with the grim reaper-like expression and thick wire-rimmed glasses seemed determined to pin that label on him.

He scooted forward in his chair, trying to pay attention and look like a mature adult because his mother was sitting right there staring at him. If there was anything he hated, it was having to account to his mother for his misdeeds.

Before any profound words could leave his throat, Ms. Henshaw removed an iPad from her briefcase and laid it on the coffee table, pushing it toward him with one long finger. She tapped the screen. A photo of a young woman appeared.

"This is Valerie Green. Are you sure you don't know her?"

He studied the pretty, blue-eyed blonde. She looked vaguely familiar, but he'd seen girls like that all over the country as he traveled the rodeo circuit. How was he supposed to remember this one?

"She's from Denver, Colorado," Ms. Henshaw added.

That triggered his memory. "Yeah, I met Valerie at a rodeo almost three years ago, I think. I'm not clear on the time. We hooked up for a wild weekend after the rodeo."

Ms. Henshaw's gray eyes skewered him above her glasses. "Hooked up? Is that your way of saying you slept with her?"

Again, Phoenix was very aware his mother was listening to every word. He was a grown man, and she knew the lifestyle he and his brother Paxton lived on the circuit. Although Paxton's life was much more colorful than his. The thought of his brother reminded him he had to be on the road in ten minutes, so he'd better get this over with.

For a moment he considered this might all be a joke. Maybe his buddies were getting him back for the times he'd played tricks on them. But one look at the grim reaper's expression and Phoenix knew the woman had never cracked a joke in her whole life.

This was serious.

"Yeah." That was the honest truth. In front of his mother. And it didn't hurt a bit.

The woman touched the screen again, and the face of a little boy popped up. Phoenix stared at the brown hair and the big brown eyes, and recognition tugged at his heart.

"That's Jake. He's Valerie's son and twenty-five months old."

Phoenix raised his eyes to stare into her steely grays. "You said you're looking for the father. I'm not the father."

In response, she touched the iPad again, and a document filled the screen. "This is a birth certificate, and if you look closely you'll see that you are listed as the father."

Oh, crap! There it was in black and white. "I spent a weekend with the woman almost three years ago. She liked rodeo cowboys and followed the circuit. If she was pregnant with my child, I'm sure she would have found a way to get in touch with me."

"If you're not the father, why do you think she would put your name on the birth certificate?"

Phoenix shrugged. "I have no idea." He rubbed his hands together, not wanting to appear callous. "What's happened to Valerie that you're now looking for the father?" The woman hadn't given any details, and he was curious.

Ms. Henshaw picked up the iPad and placed it on her lap. "I'm coordinating this case with a CPS worker in Denver. Valerie has no living relatives, and we're trying to place this little boy with relatives. Hopefully, his father."

"So Valerie's out of the picture?"

"We haven't been able to locate her. Jake lived with his great-grandmother, who had been named managing conservator since Valerie left him to get married. A week ago the great-grandmother passed away. She was found on the floor in the kitchen, and the autopsy showed she died from a brain aneurysm."

"Where was the boy?"

"This is just an assumption, but when he couldn't wake his great-grandmother, he pulled a chair to the front door and somehow opened it and got out. He was found on the street two blocks away in nothing but a soiled diaper. Someone saw him and called the police, who went door-to-door trying to find where the little boy had come from.

A neighbor identified him, and that's how they found Mrs. Green. He is now in foster care and not happy. He cries daily wanting Ma Ma."

Phoenix clasped his hands together until they were numb. The story did a number on his conscience. Could the kid be his? The question went round and round in his head like a lead marble, leaving indentions that he didn't want to feel.

"Have the police given up on finding Valerie?"

"No, but with few leads they're stumped. Mrs. Green's neighbor said that Valerie met a guy who wanted to get married, but he didn't want the kid. That's why she left him with her grandmother. The neighbor said the baby was about three months old then, and Valerie hadn't been back to see the boy since. The grandmother kept hoping she would return. The boy needed someone younger in his life."

Phoenix felt a tug on his heart again for that little boy. His emotions were getting involved, and he couldn't let that happen. The kid wasn't his.

Ms. Henshaw thumbed through the iPad. "The authorities there also talked to a friend of Valerie's. She hadn't heard from Valerie since she'd married, but when questioned about Jake, she said that Valerie didn't really know who the father was. When asked why your name was on the birth certificate, the woman said probably because it was an easy name to remember."

Oh, man. Even if this was a joke, his buddies could never get it this good or pick a woman as heartless as Valerie Green.

"The woman gave CPS two more names, and we're tracking them down. Valerie was determined to get child support from someone. That is, until the new man came along and she forgot about the boy. That may be why she never contacted you." She thumbed through more information. "The grandmother received a good pension from her husband, so the child was well taken care of. I guess Valerie knew that. Now—" she reached inside the big bag again "—it's time to find out who the father really is." She pulled out a vial with what looked like a large Q-tip in it. "If you agree, I can swab your mouth, and we'll know in a couple of weeks if you're the father or not."

A swarm of butterflies attacked his stomach, similar to when he slid onto an eighteen-hundred-pound bull, knowing this was it—the truth. He'd either get thrown onto his keister or last the eight seconds.

"Sure. I just feel I'm not the father." Yet that feeling was slowly waning.

Ms. Henshaw got up and came over to him. Within a second, she ran the swab through his mouth and placed it back into the tube. He noticed his name was written on it. That was it. Easy. The truth would be easy.

She stowed her iPad in the big briefcase and handed him a business card. "My phone numbers are on there. Call if you have any questions."

"Thanks. How will I get the results?"

She reached for her phone in her purse. "I can call you, which would probably be the easiest way since you're always on the circuit. What's your number?"

He gave it to her, and she stored it in her phone. She then turned to his mother. "Thanks, Mrs. Rebel, for allowing me into your home. I hope we can resolve this situation soon."

His mother stood and shook the woman's hand. "I hope you find the little boy's father. A boy needs a father."

"Yes, ma'am, I agree with you."

Phoenix got to his feet and also shook the woman's hand. "I'm a little conflicted about all this, but if I'm the father, I will take responsibility."

She nodded and walked toward the front door. His mother followed, and his brothers Jude and Quincy came in from the kitchen.

"What's going on?" Jude asked.

"A girl I spent a weekend with says I'm the father of her baby." Phoenix had no problem talking to his brothers. That's how they'd gotten through the years after their father's death. They shared with and depended on each other.

"Is it possible?" Quincy asked.

"Yep. She put my name on the birth certificate, but her friend said she wasn't sure who the father was. Isn't that a touching story?"

"Did you use protection?" Quincy kept up the questions.

"I always use protection."

"Then you may not be." Jude patted him on the shoulder. "Did she do a DNA test?"

"Yes." Phoenix reached for his hat on the chair. "Now you two can stop smothering me. I may be the youngest, but I'm old enough to take care of my own life, even if I screw up every now and then."

His mother joined the little group. "Did Phoenix tell you what's going on?"

"Yes, Mom, I did. And now I have to go to a rodeo. I'll let y'all know if I'm a daddy or not."

"Phoenix, I want to talk to you."

"Sorry, Mom, I've got to go." No way was he having this conversation with his mother.

Quincy was a step behind him. "We're here if you need us."

Looking back at his older brother, Phoenix knew he could depend on Quincy for anything. Jude, too. And his other brothers. They were family. But this time Phoenix had to go this alone to sort through his own thoughts and everything that had happened back then.

Phoenix nodded. "See y'all in a couple weeks." He walked out the door to the truck and travel trailer waiting in the driveway. Climbing into the passenger seat, he said, "Let's go."

Paxton shoved the shift into gear. "What's going on? What did that woman want?"

"Just drive and get us out of Horseshoe, Texas." Phoenix leaned back his head and pulled his hat over his eyes, hoping his brother would get the message. He didn't want to talk.

The three-quarter-ton truck pulled the travel trailer with ease, but the ride was still bumpy, and Phoenix's thoughts were even bumpier. He tried to remember Valerie and that time. It was a little blurry because they were drinking and having fun like he did after a lot of rodeos. Lately he and Paxton had slowed down. He hated to say it was an age thing. He preferred to look at it as maturity.

After the rodeo, Valerie and some girls had come back to the cowboy area and asked if they wanted to party. Of course, that was like asking a cowboy if he wanted beer. They went to a club and danced and drank and then went to a motel. The next night was much the same. Valerie made a beeline for him and they hooked up again. This time he sensed she was on something more than beer and figured she was just a little too wild for him. He wasn't into the heavy stuff. He was a cowboy. Riding came first with him.

She'd wanted his number, and he'd given her a fake one because he knew he didn't want to see her again. He remembered that vividly. Little things were starting to come back. Valerie was just a one-night stand. That would be sad if he was her child's father. That wasn't how children were supposed to be conceived. Oh, man.

He sat up straight and gazed out at the scenery flashing by. Rural Texas in September was still dry and hot, but the greenery was beginning to fade as signs of fall were creeping in.

"You ready to talk?" Paxton asked.

"No."

"You don't have to. I've already gotten messages from Quincy and Jude."

"They're like two mother hens."

"You got caught, huh?"

"Shut up." They rode for a while in silence and then Phoenix asked, "Do you remember Valerie Green?"

"No."

"I'm having a hard time remembering her, too, but some of it's coming back. A buckle bunny who wanted to have fun, and now she says I'm her kid's dad. And don't ask me if I used protection or I'll hit you."

"Why would I judge you? I could be in your boots."

Phoenix and Paxton had traveled the circuit for years, and they knew each other better than anyone. They liked the girls who came to the rodeos. They couldn't deny that. The women's attention was a turn-on. But now Phoenix was wondering why he needed all that attention.

"I don't feel like a father. Aren't you supposed to feel those things?"

Paxton laughed, slapping his hand against the steering wheel. "You're asking me?"

"Right. What was I thinking?" Paxton, with his charismatic charm and good looks, was the proverbial playboy. Around the rodeo circuit he was known as the "Heartthrob." Women gravitated toward him, and he had his pick of anyone he wanted. At times that had gotten him into some jams. Last year a girl wrecked his whole rodeo season, but he'd straightened up his act, and now both of them were in the top ten cowboys in the country. They would be in Vegas for the big show come December if they didn't screw up.

"You know, Pax, I'm changing my ways. It's not a good feeling for someone to come out of the blue and say I might have a son. That's irresponsible and immature. Dad would not be happy with me. From now on I will be choosy about whom I sleep with."

"Yeah, right." Paxton drove past two girls in a red Volkswagen. Once the girls saw the truck and trailer, with "Save a Horse. Ride a Cowboy." sticker they honked their horn and waved out the window. Right there, Phoenix decided the girl thing was just too easy and he had to be more responsible. He wouldn't give in to any more light flirtations.

His mind kept rolling with the miles, and he seemed to have a need to look back over his life and the rodeo. It had been one endless party, and he felt the weight of that for the first time. How could he have created a life and not know anything about it? That was unacceptable.

"Why do you think we need the excitement and attention of the rodeo?"

"Go back to sleep, Phoenix. You're giving me a headache."

"I'm serious. I think we crave the attention we got from our dad, and we get that from the rodeo and the girls."

"Don't bring Dad into this. You're agonizing over this kid and he might not even be yours. Just go to sleep and don't think about it until you get the call."

That was easy for Pax to say. He hadn't seen the face of the little boy or heard how he was crying for his great-grandma. For his own sanity, Phoenix leaned back and tried to sleep. It didn't work. In his defense, he worked as hard as he played. It took a lot of training and skill to stay on an ornery bull for eight seconds. This past year they had put in a lot of effort to accomplish their goals, including the ultimate prize—competing, and winning, at the National Finals Rodeo. Phoenix had won the gold buckle in bull riding last year, and he was hoping to repeat. Paxton was close on his heels. If he had to lose, he'd want to lose to his brother.

In Wichita Falls, they switched drivers, and Phoenix drove all the way to Oklahoma. They arrived at the rodeo grounds in the late afternoon. The rodeo was tonight, and trucks and trailers were parked everywhere. The travel trailer was much better than sleeping in the truck, which they'd done for a lot of years before they'd started to make money.

Phoenix pulled up behind a truck and trailer with stripes down the side.

"Would you look at that?"

Paxton sat up and straightened his hat. "That's a fancy outfit."

"I'm not talking about that. It's parked in two spots. That's not the cowboy way. We respect each other, and that person just hogged a parking spot."

"Park somewhere else. We have to check in."

Maybe it was his bad mood, but Phoenix decided he wasn't parking somewhere else. He was going to teach this person a lesson in manners. He pulled in as close as he could to the other rig.

"What are you doing? We're too close."

"My thought exactly. Maybe he can crawl out the window, because he's not opening the driver's side door."

It didn't take them long to find out the driver was not a he but a she. She climbed out the passenger door and stormed over to them. Phoenix got out and met her and was completely taken aback by the beauty of a woman he'd seen many times, but never this close up.

She was slim, in tight-fitting denim, boots and a white tank top tucked into her jeans…basically the sexiest woman he'd ever seen. A leather belt with a gold belt buckle she had won barrel racing circled her tiny waist. A Stetson crowned her head, and long, coppery hair hung down her back. Her eyes were the coldest blue he'd ever seen, similar to the sky when the ground was frozen on a winter's day. A chill slid up his spine.

"What do you think you're doing? Move your truck. It's too close to mine."

"You're taking up two spaces. That's not the cowboy way."

She placed her hands on her waist, stretching the tank top across full breasts. Any other time Phoenix would have enjoyed the view, but he was still in anger mode. "Excuse me?"

"We look out for each other, and taking up more space than you need is not good or respectful."

"You've got to be kidding."

"I'm not. If you want to get into your truck, you'll have to move it over."

"You…you…you despicable, conniving, egotistical…"

A smile touched his face for the first time today. This was so out of character for him. He was usually easygoing and fun to be around. He held up a hand. "I get the picture. You still have to move your truck and horse trailer. It promotes good relationships within the cowboy community."

"You may have won this round, Mr.…."

He held out his hand. "Phoenix Rebel."

She glanced at his hand and then at his face, her blue eyes now so cold he was tempted to take a step backward. "I know who you are, and I would never touch you. You Rebels are all alike, greedy, selfish and without respect for others." After saying that, she stormed back to her truck and climbed through the passenger door. In seconds she had it backed up and reparked.

Phoenix crawled back into his truck, and Paxton stared at him with a lifted eyebrow.

"Have you lost your mind? Everybody parks wherever they want. All of a sudden we have rules? No one told me."

"Shut up."

"You do know who she is?"

Phoenix rubbed his hand across the steering wheel. "Yes. Rosemary McCray."

"Rosemary McCray Wilcott," Paxton corrected him. "She's divorced, I heard."

"What else do you know about her?"

Paxton turned to face him. "Let me refresh your memory. Ezra McCray tried to kill you and Jude for jumping his fences. Jude has a bullet scar on his forehead to prove it. Our father, John Rebel, shot and killed Ezra, which escalated the Rebel/McCray feud to high alert. Rosemary is a McCray, and the off-limits sign is flashing right above her head. Don't you see it?"

"What else?" Phoenix asked again, as if Pax hadn't spoken.

Paxton sighed. "Phoenix."

"What else?"

"Her horse's name is Golden Lady, and the cowboys call Ms. Wilcott Frosty Lady because she's shot down everyone who's tried to date her."

"I know that. What else?"

"Not much. Her friends call her Rosie, but she isn't very friendly and she stays to herself, which you should do, too. Do you hear me?"

Phoenix couldn't get that look in her eyes out of his mind. "She must be younger than me, because I don't remember her in school."

"Yeah. About four years, I think." Paxton nailed him with a dark stare. "Why are you curious?"

"I don't know. There's just something about her. She seems so sad."

"Is that why you laid into her like a crazy fool?"

"I didn't know it was her. I thought it was a guy."

"Oh, that makes sense. Someone who could punch your lights out. Right before a rodeo, I might add."

Phoenix tapped his fingers on the steering wheel. "What else do you know about her?"

Paxton groaned. "You're not going to let this go, are you?"

"I'm curious. That's all."

"I heard down at Rowdy's beer joint that Ira McCray married her off to a man twice her age. The man was supposed to pour money into the McCray ranch to get it back on its feet. Rosemary filed for divorce a year later and Ira disowned her. I'd say not being able to see your family is a lot to be sad about."

"Yeah." Phoenix felt a stab of guilt for being so rude to her. It was just a reflex reaction to everything that was going on in his life. He didn't want to be taken advantage of anymore.

Paxton opened his door. "Do you want to set up the trailer or check us in?"

Phoenix got out of the truck. "I'll check us in." As he passed Rosemary's vehicle, he thought of going over and apologizing to her. But he knew the last thing she wanted from him was an apology. She wanted revenge, and in the days that followed she would probably find a way to get back at him.

## Chapter Two

Rosie sat on the small sofa in her live-in horse trailer, willing the anger to subside. The trucks and trailers were parked in a field close to the rodeo arena. There were no marked spots. How dare he chastise her for taking up space? How dare he!

In a hurry because Dixie, her precious Jack Russell–mixed terrier, had to pee, she'd pulled in quickly, not noticing she was far away from the other vehicle. She'd opened the door and Dixie had hopped out to do her business. Then Phoenix Rebel had the nerve to pull in so close she couldn't get out of her truck. Who did he think he was?

She'd seen him and his brother Paxton many times at the rodeos. She ignored them and they ignored her. It worked well considering their family histories. Until today. She should have refused to move her truck, but escalating a feud that should've died years ago was not one of her goals. She preferred a quiet, peaceful life, but bending to his will grated on her nerves.

The times she'd seen him around the rodeo, he was always laughing and joking with the cowboys, and some girl was always hanging off his arm. Today was a complete about-face from the guy she'd glimpsed on occasion.

He'd lost his cool and she had no idea why. The parking couldn't have been it. Was he just trying to get in a dig at her because she was a McCray? She didn't care anymore. She was going to forget about the whole thing because she intended to ride very well at this rodeo. Her scores were good, and going to Vegas was her main goal. Her livelihood depended on how well she rode and how much money she'd make. And Phoenix Rebel was not going to break her stride.

Dixie whined and Rosie picked her up, stroking her. Dixie and Golden Lady, her palomino horse, were her family now. And that was just too sad even to think about. Her father had said she could never come home because she had betrayed the family. But living a lonely life was better than living the life her father had planned for her. She shook the memories away, refusing to let them get her down. She had to prepare for the rodeo.

A tap sounded at the door, and she jumped. It couldn't be. Tentatively she got to her feet and opened the door. Haley Wilson stood there. A barrel racer, Rosie saw her at the rodeos and they'd become friendly. Rosie usually kept to herself, but Haley was outgoing and bubbly and sometimes wouldn't take no for an answer.

"Hey, I saw your trailer. You riding tonight?" With brown hair and brown eyes, Haley was a typical cowgirl with tight jeans, an equally tight shirt, boots and a Stetson. And a smile that stretched all the way to Austin.

"Yeah. Come in." She never asked anyone into her living quarters, but today she did for some reason. Maybe that lonely thing was getting to her.

Haley looked around. "This is nice. Mine is much smaller, and I'm always happy to get home to my comfy bed, aren't you?"

Rosie couldn't tell her this was her home and comfy bed. This was where she lived full-time because she couldn't afford anything else. Luckily Haley kept talking, so a response wasn't necessary.

"When I start winning money, I'm upgrading big time." Haley scratched Dixie's head. "What a cutie."

"She's my roommate."

Haley thumbed over her shoulder. "Isn't that the Rebel boys' trailer next to you?"

"Yeah. You got a thing for the Rebels?"

"Well, I wouldn't say no if they asked me out for a beer."

Why were women such suckers? The Rebel boys only wanted one thing. But if Haley was willing, what business was it of Rosie's?

Haley turned toward the door. "I gotta get my horse over to the arena. I'll see you there. Good luck tonight."

"You, too."

Rosie slipped on a white sparkly Western shirt and tucked it into her jeans. At the arena, she would wrap Lady's legs below the knee with white also. It was a thing with her to match, and her fans had come to expect it. She kissed Dixie goodbye and went out to the trailer to unload Lady.

When Rosie had first seen the palomino with the white mane and tail, she'd known she had to have her. She was a beautiful horse and she had speed unlike any horse Rosie had ever owned. Stroking her gently, Rosie cooed silly words to her, making sure no one could hear, especially Phoenix Rebel.

In minutes she had a saddle on her and was ready to ride over to the arena. With one boot in the stirrup, she noticed Phoenix coming out of his trailer.

"Can I talk to you for a minute?" His voice was soft now with an underlying tone of huskiness, but it did nothing for her. She didn't like the man.

"I have nothing to say to you. Now or ever. But I do hope the bull you ride tonight has big horns and points them south where the sun don't shine." She kneed Lady and rode away, enjoying the stunned look on his face.

PHOENIX GAVE UP trying to apologize to a woman who was as stubborn as a mule. He did enjoy her sense of humor, though. She could be his kind of woman except for one thing: she was a McCray and he was a Rebel. And that other thing, too. She hated his guts.

He didn't know why he was thinking about her when he had enough on his plate to keep him occupied for the next few months. She ignored him for the rest of the rodeo and again when she saw him in Pasadena, Texas. The ignoring thing went on. Sometimes, just to annoy her, he would walk her way to see if she would react. She didn't. They met up again in Tyler. The ignoring thing was set in stone.

By then, Phoenix was focused on his phone. He checked it at least twenty-five times a day to see if Ms. Henshaw had called. He thought of calling her but decided against that. He'd just wait in la-la land until the big moment.

In Tyler, Phoenix drew a bull called Buster, named because he busted cowboys' scores. Paxton had ridden two rides ahead of him on Rough Stuff and had scored an eighty-six.

The bull was in the chute, snorting and angry, but the chute held him tight. It was time to ride. Phoenix adjusted the chaps that Jude had made for him and then worked on his spurs. Paxton was known for his red shirts, but Phoenix was known for his colorful plaid shirts. His protective vest was black, and he slipped his arms into the holes and got comfortable in it.

When he heard his name, he walked to the chute, climbed up and checked his bull rope. The stench of bull and urine filled his nostrils. At this point his stomach started to churn, and it took a moment for the feeling to subside. The stands were full tonight with eager, noisy fans. The bright lights beamed onto the arena. A hush came over the crowd as he eased on to the back of the huge, muscled, angry bull, who snorted and moved restlessly. Phoenix felt the enormous power beneath him, sucked air into his lungs and adjusted the braided bull rope to get the feel that he needed. With his glove on, he worked his hand into the handle on the rope.

Pax was on the chute to help him. "Have you got a good grip?"

"I got it."

*This is for you, Dad.* He said that to himself before every ride.

He raised his left arm and nodded. The gate flung open, and Buster jumped head-down into the arena, kicking out with his back legs and going into a spin. Phoenix held on, his mind whirling as he counted in his head. Eight seconds always felt like thirty. He maintained his position, even spurring the bull so he would jump higher. At the buzzer he leaped off, stumbled and rolled toward the fence. The bullfighters had Buster headed toward the open gate.

He got to his feet, picked up his hat and waited for the score. Eighty-five. Damn. He'd expected it to be higher. That was the nature of riding.

The rodeo came to an end on Saturday night. Paxton and Phoenix placed first and second. It had been a long season and they would finish out in October before Vegas, just to keep practicing and maintaining their skill. They'd worked a lot of years to get to this point. It could all go wrong in a second, though.

At the arena, the cowboys were packing up, getting ready to move on to another rodeo. Eden, their brother Falcon's daughter, had joined them. She was in college, but she barrel-raced occasionally.

"Hey, y'all going out to party tonight?" Cole Bryant, another bull rider, asked.

"You bet," Paxton told him. "We're taking Eden out for the evening."

"If Eden's going, then I'm coming, too."

Phoenix threw an arm across Cole's shoulder. "You touch my niece and I'll have to hurt you."

Cole held up his hands. "Okay. I got it, but why don't you let her make up her own mind?"

"And why don't I just punch you in the face?"

"Come on, guys." Paxton got between them. "It's Saturday night. Let's have some fun."

Eden, pretty as a picture with dark hair and green eyes, walked up. "Where are we going tonight?" She wiggled her hips. "I'm eager to dance, especially with my uncs."

Rosemary strolled by, leading her horse and not casting an eye their way. There was just something about her that drew Phoenix's attention. A sadness that he could feel, which was crazy. He must have hit his head in the arena.

"One of these days, I'm going to ride as good as her," Eden said.

Before anyone could respond, Phoenix's phone buzzed. He pulled it out of his pocket and froze as he saw the name. Ms. Henshaw. "Excuse me. I have to take this." He walked to the fence and leaned against the pipe railing.

"Ms. Henshaw?"

"Mr. Rebel, I have news for you."

"You have the results from the DNA test?"

"Yes."

He sucked in a deep breath as if he was going to ride the meanest bull in the world. "What are they?"

"You're the father. Ninety-nine point nine, and that's as close as you can get. There's no doubt."

He slid down the fence like a drunk who'd had one too many. Sitting there on the ground, with the smell of the manure and the animals of the rodeo around him, he suddenly knew his life had just changed. Fun-loving Phoenix would be no more. He had to be a responsible, mature adult now. He had to be a father.

"Mr. Rebel, are you there?"

"Yes, ma'am." Off in the distance, he could see the moon casting a beam that seemed to guide him toward the future, whatever that might be. But it would include a little boy named Jake.

"Did you mean what you said that day I met with you at your home?"

"What was that?"

"That you would take responsibility."

Phoenix closed his eyes, and in his mind he could hear his father's voice. *Always take responsibility.* Like Jude and Falcon, who had also become fathers unexpectedly, he would never do anything to dishonor his father. "Yes, ma'am. I will take responsibility for my son. What do I do now?"

"Are you sure about this? The CPS worker in Denver told me she has two couples who want the little boy."

All the doubts in his mind vanished. "No. Jake belongs to me, and I will take full responsibility for him. What do I have to do?"

"Tomorrow is Sunday, but I'll meet you in my office in Austin in the morning. Jake needs to be with his family as soon as possible. I will give you the papers you'll need and you will fly to Denver. Make plane reservations as soon as you can. There will be a hearing before a judge on Monday morning. Valerie Green's maternal rights will be terminated and you will be granted full custody. The CPS worker there will meet you and you can visit with Jake. After the hearing, you can bring him home and he will be legally yours."

"I can do that. Give me the address of your office. Oh, wait. I don't have a pen. Just text it to me."

"Okay. I will also text a list of things you will need for the little boy, like a bed, diapers, milk and such. Have you ever been around children?"

"Yes, some of my brothers have children. So I do have some experience."

"Very good. I will send you a text in case you want to pick up some things tonight, and I will see you tomorrow."

"Thank you, Ms. Henshaw."

He sat there in the warmth of the night, staring at his phone. He didn't have to wait any longer. He was Jake's father. How could that be? How could he also not know about it? How could he be so irresponsible? A lot of his family members could answer that before he could snap his fingers. Yep, he was about to pay for his upbringing.

Paxton and Eden came over. "What are you doing sitting there on the ground?" Paxton asked. "Let's go."

"I have to go home."

Paxton and Eden stared at each other, and then they sank down beside him. "Should I say congratulations or I'm sorry?" Paxton grimaced.

"I'm not sure," he admitted. "But I'm that little boy's father, and now I have to live up to the title."

Eden put her arm around his shoulders. "You're going to make a great father. You're a big kid yourself."

"I feel as if I've aged ten years in five minutes." He tried to get to his feet and realized his legs were shaky. This was harder than any fall he'd ever taken. He felt bruised, weak and disoriented.

Once on his feet, he said, "I'm going home tonight. I have to make arrangements for tomorrow. But you guys stay and party."

"No way." Eden hugged him. "We're all going home. We're family."

Phoenix didn't have any strength to argue. His mind was solely on his son and the days ahead. How would he handle this new development in his life? He wasn't known for maturity.

They loaded up and headed out, Eden leading with her truck and trailer. Paxton drove and Phoenix made plane reservations on his phone. He got a flight to Denver at eleven in the morning. That didn't give him much time to meet with Ms. Henshaw, but he wouldn't be able to sleep tonight anyway, so he would be there early.

Ms. Henshaw's text came through and he just stared at all the things that he needed to buy. Diapers. He had a weak stomach. How was he going to change diapers? This was a situation where he really had to cowboy up.

They didn't talk much on the drive home. Phoenix's thoughts were all turned inward. He wasn't a worrier by nature, but worries jabbed at him like the fists of a prizefighter. Would he make a good father? He had to. It wasn't a question. It was fact now.

He leaned back his head and tried to sleep. But all he could think about was that little boy who was crying for his great-grandma. A little boy who had been let down by a reckless, immature father. And an equally reckless, immature mother. Phoenix had to make up for all of that.

It was a three-hour drive, and Phoenix had never been so glad to see the ranch. In the wee hours of the morning, they drove up to the barn. After unloading her horse, Eden went toward her parents' house, and Paxton and Phoenix walked toward the bunkhouse.

On the way, Phoenix kept thinking about the list on his phone. He needed to have those things here when he brought Jake home.

"I'm going into Temple to buy a baby bed."

Paxton stopped on the porch of the bunkhouse, his eyebrows knotted together in confusion. "What? Where can you buy a bed at this time of the morning?"

"Walmart Supercenter. They're open twenty-four hours."

"Don't you think you need to rest?"

"I won't be able to sleep until I can bring Jake home where he belongs."

Paxton sighed. "Okay. I'll go with you."

Phoenix shook his head. "I don't need you to go with me. I can buy a bed all by myself. Just go to sleep. I'll see you in the morning."

"Phoenix…"

He looked at the brother he'd spent most of his life

with and saw the concern and worry in his eyes. "I'm struggling. Okay." He was as honest as he could be because he couldn't be anything else at this point. "I have to be there for that little boy. Do you understand?"

Paxton nodded, and Phoenix headed for his truck. Shopping early in the morning meant there was hardly anyone in the store. Clerks were stocking shelves and a few people were strolling around. He found the baby section and stared at all the clothes and paraphernalia. Where were the baby beds? He found them on another aisle. Again he just stared. What kind did he need? Maybe he should've brought Paxton. At least the two of them could have figured out something. But this shouldn't be difficult. A bed was a bed.

Or so he'd thought. They came with or without a mattress and in numerous colors from white to espresso to black. In different styles. His head began to spin. Clearly he needed help.

He turned to search for a clerk and ran into someone. "Oh, sorry. I wasn't looking where I was going." He caught the woman's arm and just stared, unable to believe his eyes.

Rosemary McCray Wilcott stared right back at him with a look of shock that was echoed in his eyes.

What was she doing in Walmart at this time of the morning?

# Chapter Three

"Uh…"

Rosie was stunned, and she could neither speak a coherent word nor move. The last person she'd expected to run into in Walmart was Phoenix Rebel. It took a full thirty seconds for her to regain her cool. In that time she was very aware of the hand holding her elbow. The firm, callused fingers were gentle and comforting, and that threw her more than seeing him. She didn't want to feel anything for this man. Very slowly she removed her elbow and licked her suddenly dry lips.

She'd come in the store only for a few minutes because she was out of Dixie's treats. The dog would whine and whine until she got them. Also, Rosie had received some unsettling news and couldn't sleep anyway. She rented ten acres with a barn and corral, where she parked her trailer. Mrs. Boyd, the owner, had called and said her daughter was moving back home and was thinking of building a house on the property. That meant Rosie would have to find another place to park her trailer and another home for Lady. Her lease was up at the first of the year so that gave her a few months, but she'd been hoping to buy the place herself one day. Now she had to change her plans.

Whenever she was in Walmart, she couldn't resist strolling to the baby section. It was gut-wrenching, but cathartic in a way for her loss of her little girl. One day, maybe, she could stop reliving the painful memories.

"I'm sorry. Did I hurt you?" Phoenix asked.

His strong tones brought her back to the present and the embarrassing situation. "No." She made to walk off because she had nothing else to say to him.

"Hey."

Against her better judgment, she looked back. "Am I taking up too much space?"

"I deserve that." The corners of his mouth lifted in a cockamamy grin, which she was sure worked wonders on the opposite sex. To her dismay it was working on her, too.

She'd never seen a more handsome cowboy than Phoenix, and she hated that she noticed. In tight Wranglers, boots and a plaid shirt, he was every girl's dream. The strong, carved facial bones that showcased a perpetual smile only added to the masculine mix. As did the Stetson and the riot of dark hair that always peeped out from under it.

"I'm really sorry for being rude in Oklahoma. I was having a very bad day."

The apology put a dent in her already shaky composure. *Walk away. Walk away.* The words kept running through her mind, but her feet wouldn't move as she stared into his dark eyes. Dark, warm, smiling eyes.

"I'm looking for a baby bed, and I could really use some help. Are you up for the job?" He tilted his head slightly, and the teasing light in his eyes did a number on her control.

Again, against her better judgment, she asked, "Why would you need a baby bed?"

"Well, you see, I just found out I'm a father."

"Oh." His honesty threw her, and her curiosity spiked. "And you get to be a weekend father?"

"No. Full-time."

"You're getting custody of a baby?"

The light in his eyes turned up a notch. "Yeah. Go figure."

She gave up trying to make herself leave. He needed help with baby stuff, and there was nothing she would love more. It would hurt. But she just loved the punishment, she supposed.

"Girl or boy?"

"Boy." He gave a thumbs-up sign.

"You must be excited." At that, her guard went down so far she could no longer see it.

Suddenly a look of resignation crossed his face. "I would be lying if I said I was excited out of my mind. It's been a shock and I'm trying to adjust. He's twenty-five months old."

She could have said a lot of petty things about the cowboys and the buckle bunnies around the rodeo, but she saw the hurt in his eyes. "Is the mother out of the picture?"

"Yeah. She left the boy with her grandmother and the grandmother has passed away. CPS tracked down the father, which happens to be me."

Rosie didn't know what else to say. It had to have been a big shock, and he seemed to be taking it well. She glanced at the row of baby beds. "If he's twenty-five months old, you probably need something you can convert into a toddler bed." She pointed to a box that had a picture on it. "See, there's one. It goes from baby to toddler."

"That looks perfect."

She walked over to several boxes. "There are different colors. Maybe dark chocolate or warm honey. Which do you prefer?"

"Warm honey. Every time."

She ignored the hidden reference to her in his voice. But it made her very aware of her attire: sweatpants, flip-flops and an old T-shirt. Her long hair was loose, and she brushed it away from her face in a nervous gesture. "They...they'll probably have to load this into your truck, so it probably would be best to just take a picture with your phone and show them at checkout."

"Now, see, that's why women are best at this. They cover all the angles." He took a quick photo and then looked at something on the phone. "I have to get a car seat, and she gave me the brand name."

"She?"

"The CPS worker."

"Oh. And you'll need sheets, too."

He looked at his phone again. "She didn't say anything about sheets."

Men! "Are you going to let him sleep on the bare mattress?"

That smile was back in place and it was lethal. "Okay, sheets it is."

"They're in the next aisle." He followed her around the corner with his cart. They looked like a normal couple out shopping early in the morning. But they would never be a couple. "Here they are." She squatted to glance through them. "There are ones with duckies, horses, dogs and..."

"Horses."

"And cartoon characters…"

"Horses."

"Oh, look at these John Deere ones."

"Horses."

"And there are solid colors…" She held up her hand before he could say the word. "I know—horses."

"Well, he's my kid and I like horses so he'll like horses."

She pulled three sets off the shelf. "You are in for a what-have-I-gotten-myself-into moment." She stood and handed him the sheets.

Placing them in the cart, he asked, "Why do I need so many?"

"Think, cowboy. It's a baby and babies pee. A lot. So you need extras in case of an accident."

He reached down and grabbed two more.

After that, he followed her around the store and listed off everything on his phone. His cart was stacked high with diapers. There wasn't room for one more thing. Actually he couldn't even see over it.

And then they were in the toy section because he wanted to get a toy for the baby. As she walked by all the baby dolls her throat closed. It had been almost nine years and still the pain was as raw and new as the day they'd told her that her baby was dead. She stopped and stared at a doll with reddish-blond hair and couldn't look away. She was trying not to remember. Not to feel. Not to act like a complete fool.

"I don't think he'll like that." Phoenix's words brought her out of her trance. She didn't quite make it on the fool part because she felt sure he thought she was crazy.

"Boys play with dolls." She tried to cover up the embarrassing moment.

"Not my boy."

"Oh, please. Don't tell me you're going to be one of those fathers."

He walked past her to the boy section, ignoring her words. "Now we're talking." He picked up a truck and trailer with horses. "My kid will love this."

"You know, you're under the impression this little boy is going to be just like you. Sometimes it doesn't turn out that way. I'm not an expert, but I'm right on this."

He didn't fire any heated words back at her. He just stared down at the truck and trailer in his hands. "Yeah. I know nothing about the kid, but I hope I find a part of me in him."

"You haven't met him?" She couldn't hide the shock in her words.

"No. I'm flying out to Denver tomorrow to pick him up and to meet him."

She had no words and she wanted to ask questions, but she felt it was time to put an end to this unexpected interlude. She didn't want to get involved in his life, and she didn't want to know any more about him and his son.

"I have to go. I wish you the very best with your little boy."

He looked into her eyes, and once again she felt the warmth all the way to her heart. "Thanks. May I call you Rosie?"

She shook her head. "You and I will never be on a first-name basis. Tonight was just a time out of time that neither one of us expected and will never be repeated. You know the reasons why."

"Come on. That's not fair. You're not even a McCray anymore."

"I was born a McCray and I will always be a McCray."

"I might need more help…"

She wasn't falling for that again. "Goodbye. I'll see you around the rodeos." Walking away, she felt something she couldn't quite describe. Being lonely was just a part of her, but tonight, for a brief moment, she'd felt something special with a man she didn't even like. She'd felt like a woman again. It was hard to describe since all they'd done was talk. Phoenix Rebel probably didn't even want the child, but she had to admire that he was making the best of it. She would never be lucky enough to get a chance at having another child. The rest of her days, she would spend alone. But tonight she felt the wonder of it all because she couldn't resist his dark, warm eyes.

IT WAS ALMOST 3:00 a.m. when Phoenix drove into the yard at the bunkhouse. He left everything in the truck and went inside. The door was never locked and he didn't think anyone had a key. He was dog-tired and needed sleep. After removing his boots and belt, he fell across the bed and welcomed the blackness of his mind. But a face was there that he couldn't shake.

*Rosemary McCray's.*

He was just so shocked to see her, and when she actually melted a little and helped him, he got lost in her feminine presence. She had to be the most beautiful woman he'd ever seen. For those cowboys who called her Frosty, all he could say was, tough luck. They never saw her with her blue eyes sparkling and her hair all around her. Tonight it was loose, not a band, ribbon or anything in it. In his mind, he could see her that way when she went to bed. In nothing but her hair. Oh yeah, he could get lost in that dream. Or maybe a fantasy, because that was all Rosemary McCray could ever be to him.

She'd told him so.

PHOENIX WOKE UP at 5:30 a.m., showered and changed clothes. Today he put on a white shirt because it was a special occasion. He was going to meet his son.

Jericho, a ranch hand who lived with Phoenix and Paxton in the bunkhouse, was in the kitchen, cooking breakfast. "Just in time," he said.

Phoenix grabbed a glass of orange juice. He had OJ first thing every morning. It was a ritual for him, and he always carried a large carton on the road. Stuffing bacon into a biscuit, he said, "This is all I have time for. I have to go over to the house to see Mom."

He thought about the supplies in his truck and he quickly unloaded everything into his room. Rico helped him with the bed. Rico never asked any questions, and Phoenix loved that about the man. He never interfered with other people's business, and he didn't judge anyone.

"I'll have to put it together when I get back."

"It will be done when you bring the boy home," Rico said.

Evidently Paxton had told Rico about Jake. And now he had to tell his mother.

"Thanks, Rico. I appreciate that, but you don't have to."

"No problem." The older man shook his head. If Phoenix had to guess the man's age, he would have said somewhere in his late thirties. A scary figure to some, with his long, dark hair tied into a ponytail at his neck and a scar slashed across his face from gang fighting in Houston, he was the best friend the Rebel family ever had. He would do anything for them and they would do anything for him, too.

QUINCY'S TRUCK WAS at their mother's. That surprised Phoenix because his brother usually spent his Sunday mornings with his wife, Jenny. As he opened the back door, he heard voices. Quincy and Grandpa were drinking coffee and eating breakfast. Jude and his new wife, Paige, and their son Zane lived in the house. But no one else was up yet.

Every time he stepped into this warm kitchen, he thought of his dad and felt at home. At peace. And then the sadness would creep in like a thief in the night, threatening to steal away those emotions. But all he had to do was look at the kitchen his dad had painstakingly built for his mother, from the large tiles on the floor to the knotty pine cabinets to the dark granite with a touch of red. His dad had given special attention to detail here, just as he had with the raising of his sons. He'd taught them so much, and yet there was still so much to learn. But he wasn't here anymore, and Phoenix never felt that more deeply than today. He would take full responsibility for his child not only because he wanted to but also because his dad would have expected it of him.

He cleared his throat. "Morning, everyone."

His mother turned from the stove. "Phoenix, I didn't expect you this early. You and Paxton don't usually come in until late Sunday. Sit down. I'll get you a cup of coffee."

"No, thanks. I've already had breakfast." He glanced at his brother and Grandpa. "Why are y'all up so early?"

"I got up early to fix Grandpa's breakfast and then decided to come over and eat with Mom," Quincy explained. Elias, another brother, lived with Grandpa and usually spent Saturday nights down at Rowdy's beer joint. Grandpa was getting a little senile, and they refused to let him use the stove anymore since he almost burned the house down twice. Elias usually looked after Grandpa unless he went out for the evening. Then Quincy took up the slack because he was a big mother hen to everyone.

Quincy eyed Phoenix's starched shirt. "Where are you going all dressed up at this hour?"

Phoenix looked down at the hat in his hand and saw no reason not to tell the truth. "Ms. Henshaw called and had the DNA results. I'm the father and I'm going to Denver to pick up my son."

"What? When did you get this news?" his mother asked with a lifted eyebrow.

"Last night."

"And you're just now telling me?"

"I didn't want to do it over the phone. Besides, I had a lot of things to do like buying stuff that Jake will need. I left it all in my room, but I'll sort through it when I come back."

His mother removed her apron. "I'm going with you. You'll need a woman to help you."

"No." Phoenix held up his hand. "I'm going alone. This is my child and I will handle it. I don't need help."

"Now that's just silly, Phoenix."

Quincy stood. "I'll go. Someone needs to be with you. I'll run home and tell Jenny."

"I'm only going to say this one more time. I'm going alone. I do not need anyone to hold my hand. I've accepted that Jake is my son, and we need time to bond."

They stared at him with shocked eyes, and he supposed he did sound grown up. He'd finally made that transformation, and he wasn't sure if he liked it or not. He'd rather have been joking and teasing everyone. But those days were in his past now.

"Proud of you, boy. You've become a man." Grandpa

took a sip of his coffee. "Do you remember when your dad had the girls and sex talk with you boys?"

"Of course."

"Well, then, I would just like to know where you, Jude and Falcon were during his delivery because, obviously, you didn't hear a word. Were y'all hiding in the closet or something?"

"Abe, for heaven's sake, eat your breakfast." His mom was quick to chastise their grandfather. The two barely tolerated each other, something that had been going on ever since Phoenix could remember. It was hard on all of them, but they adjusted to the tension between their mother and their grandfather.

"Condoms are not one hundred percent safe," Phoenix said.

Grandpa took another sip of coffee. "Now, I could tell some stories about that."

"Later, Abe."

Grandpa glared at their mother, and Phoenix thought it was time for him to leave. "I'll call when I'm headed home."

"When will that be?" his mother asked.

"I'm hoping late Monday, but like I said, I will let you know. See y'all later." He headed for the door, and his mother followed him.

"Son…"

His brothers said that Phoenix was the favorite because he was the baby, and he realized for the first time today that they were right. His mother was having a hard time letting go. He didn't want to hurt her feelings, but he had to be blunt.

He looked into her worried brown eyes. "I'm okay, Mom. Please understand I have to do this alone." He hugged her briefly, kissed her cheek and walked out the door to the new life that awaited him.

HE MADE IT to Austin in time to meet with Ms. Henshaw, and they went over the legalities of the situation and what he was to expect in Denver. Then he was on his way to the airport. The two-hour flight wasn't bad, but it seemed to drag. He was eager to get there and to meet the boy who would now become part of his life.

Besides Jake, thoughts of Rosie occupied his mind. She was so different last night. *Lovable* and *likable* were words that came to mind. He couldn't stop thinking about her and wondered where she lived. Probably close to Temple, where the Walmart was. What did it matter? He and Rosie had no future. He had enough to deal with without getting involved with a McCray. He'd told himself that many times since the encounter in Oklahoma, but his thoughts always winged back to her.

There was something about her expression when she was staring at the doll. Sadness mixed with a resignation she was trying to hide. He sensed she wanted to reach out and touch it and she was forcing herself not to. Why was she so mesmerized by the doll? There had to be a reason, and against every sane thought in his head, he wanted to find out why.

The plane landed at the Denver airport and his focus turned to Jake. The way it had to be.

Rosie McCray was just a passing fantasy.

# Chapter Four

After landing at Denver International Airport, Phoenix called the number Ms. Henshaw had given him. Ms. Bauer, the Colorado CPS case worker, picked him up outside the terminal. She was much younger than Ms. Henshaw, somewhere in her thirties, with a friendly smile. Her blond hair was pinned back, and her blue eyes reminded him of someone else. He wondered if Rosie was thinking about him as much as he was thinking about her. Probably not.

Phoenix always enjoyed the Mile High City. Because of its elevation, some cowboys had breathing problems here, but Phoenix never did. The weather was a pleasant eighty degrees, and Ms. Bauer said it would get down into the low forties by morning. It was nice compared with the heat he'd left behind in Texas. They passed the stadium where the Denver Broncos played. Phoenix had almost forgotten football season had started.

Ms. Bauer drove to the foster home where Jake was staying. It was in a nice residential area with small brick houses. She parked behind an SUV in the driveway.

"Jake is a sweet little boy, but he has some problems," Ms. Bauer said before getting out of the car.

"What do you mean?"

"You have to understand that he's grieving. We're all very patient with him. There are four other kids in the house, and he hits when he doesn't get his way. 'No' is his favorite word. He's also a runner."

"A runner?"

"Yes. If he can get a door open, he's gone. Mr. and Mrs. Devers are in their late fifties, and it's hard for them to catch him. Tom, Mr. Devers, has put latches high on the doors so he can't get out. We think he's searching for his great-grandmother, and we believe he will settle down once he's in a stable environment again."

Phoenix hoped so, too. It was just like Rosie had said. He was in a what-have-I-gotten-myself-into kind of moment. But he would stand by his kid no matter what. He unfolded his body from the compact car.

"Since the Devers have four other children, we have to respect their privacy."

"Of course. I just want to see my son."

They walked up to the front door, and Ms. Bauer rang the bell. It opened to a middle-aged woman with graying brown hair holding a baby.

"Oh, Ms. Bauer, it's good to see you. Come in."

Phoenix followed Ms. Bauer into a large living area cluttered with toys. Through double windows he could see two older boys playing in the backyard. But his eyes were riveted on a little boy and a little girl sitting on the carpet playing with trucks.

"Mrs. Devers, this is Mr. Rebel, Jake's father."

The woman juggled the baby onto her shoulder and shook his hand. "It's nice to meet you. Jake really needs someone. He's been a handful crying for his great-grandmother. He just seems very unhappy."

Phoenix twisted his hat in his hand. "May I go over and speak to him?" It seemed odd asking to speak to his own son. He was willing to follow the rules, though.

"Sure. Just don't be surprised if he doesn't respond."

"I'll wait here," Ms. Bauer said.

Phoenix placed his hat on the arm of the sofa, walked over and squatted beside the boy and the girl. At that moment the little girl took the truck from Jake and he shouted, "No!" and yanked it back. "Mine," he added.

Phoenix had no idea what to say. Words were useless. He would be just another person saying something Jake didn't understand. He had to go with his gut feeling. The problem was, his gut was saying, *Run like hell.* But he stayed rooted to the spot because when he'd said he'd take responsibility, he'd meant it.

Phoenix watched his son. Even thinking the word *son* seemed foreign to him, but he would adjust. Jake's little hands clutched the truck. His dark hair was tousled across his forehead. He needed a haircut. He wore pull-up pants and a T-shirt, and his feet were bare. Phoenix stared at his toes. Phoenix's toes were shaped the same way—slanted. It was a small thing, but maybe it was what he'd been looking for, a clue to show him this little boy was his.

The girl grabbed the toy again, and Jake hit her. "No!" Jake shouted.

Without thinking, Phoenix grabbed his hand before he could hit her again. "No. We don't hit girls."

Narrowed eyes glared at him, and Jake's face scrunched into a frown.

Phoenix reached out, picked him up and then got to his feet, carrying him to the sofa. Sitting down with Jake on his lap, he waited for the frown to disappear. It didn't.

"Do you know what *daddy* means?"

Jake pointed to the girl.

"She has a daddy?" he asked Jake, but Mrs. Devers answered.

"Yes, Allie has a daddy. He comes to visit all the time and is trying to gain custody of her and her older brother, who is playing outside. Jake knows what *daddy* means."

Jake stared back at him, the frown not so intense now.

"I'm your daddy. Do you understand that, Jake?"

Jake's eyes never wavered from Phoenix's, but he didn't say anything.

Phoenix touched Jake's chest. "You're Jake." Then he touched his own chest. "I'm Daddy."

The little girl came over. "Daddy."

"No!" Jake shouted again. Yep, *no* was his favorite word.

"Allie, come with me." Mrs. Devers quickly took her hand and led her into the kitchen. Jake scrambled down and picked up the truck and a stuffed brown-and-white dog with floppy ears that was lying on the floor. He came back and crawled onto Phoenix's lap, the dog tucked under one arm and the truck in his hand.

"You like trucks?"

Jake nodded.

"I live on a big ranch and we have trucks, horses and cattle. Big trucks that you can ride in. Would you like to ride in a truck?"

Phoenix continued to talk about nonsensical things and Jake just listened. Finally, Jake rested against Phoenix's chest, and Phoenix lost his breath at the emotions that filled him. Protective. Overpowering. Parental emotions that he hadn't even known he possessed. He just wanted to make Jake's world better and safer. He wanted Jake to be happy.

Mrs. Devers and Ms. Bauer walked over. Phoenix had lost track of time and he realized it was getting late.

"Mrs. Devers said if you'd like to spend the night with Jake, you're welcome to. She can move the children around for the night. They love playing camp-out."

"Thank you, but I don't want to put you out."

"It's no problem," Mrs. Devers said. "It's important that Jake bonds with you before you take him home."

It was settled. Tom Devers came in from the grocery store, and Phoenix met him. It was a lively bunch when the kids all came to the table. Jake was very quiet, sitting in his high chair. He kept looking at Phoenix.

Later, he gave Jake a bath while Mrs. Devers watched and gave instructions, which he was glad about because he wanted to do the right things.

"I have a weak stomach," Phoenix admitted as he put a diaper on Jake.

"Then you need to do it fast, like bull riding." She grinned at him. "Yeah, I did some checking on you. I always do that when parents take kids from my home. I want to make sure they're well taken care of. Jake is still on a bottle, and he needs to be weaned from it soon and potty trained. Mr. Rebel, you have your work cut out for you."

Phoenix was going to have to learn to do a lot of things besides bull riding and ranching. They wouldn't be pleasant, either. But he would learn. With Jake tucked into bed with his dog, which Phoenix learned was called Floppy, and his favorite blanket, Phoenix removed his clothes and slipped beneath the sheet on the twin bed. He thought he wouldn't sleep because so much was crowding in on him about how his life was changing. But he fell into a deep sleep. The next thing he knew, a little hand touched his face.

"Dad-dy."

Tears stung the backs of Phoenix's eyes, and he pulled his son into his side, dog and all, and covered them with the sheet and blanket. He went to sleep holding his child, and it was the most natural feeling in the world. He would remember the moment for the rest of his life when his son had called him daddy for the first time.

A stench woke him and he knew what it was—Jake had a dirty diaper. Oh, man.

"Mr. Rebel," Mrs. Devers called from the hallway, and Phoenix quickly slipped into his jeans.

"Yes, ma'am."

Mrs. Devers appeared in the doorway. "Are you and Jake ready for breakfast?"

"Yes, ma'am," Phoenix thumbed toward Jake in bed, who was looking at him with big eyes. "He got out of his bed this morning."

"Oh, yeah. He climbs right out of it. That's why Tom put latches on all the doors. You'll have to do the same."

"Okay." He wrinkled his nose. "He has a dirty diaper."

Mrs. Devers started pulling out things and laying them on the bed. "This is a plastic bag to put it in when you re-move the diaper. Helps keep the smell down." She pointed to a trash can in the corner. "That contains another bag you put the small bag in. You can get these anyplace that sells baby supplies. I will give you a few to get you started. You need to change the big bag every day." She looked at him, and he realized she was expecting him to do something—like change the kid's diaper. Oh, man.

"Hold your breath, Mr. Rebel. It will be over before you know it."

He unsnapped Jake's pajamas between his legs, and the smell made his stomach roil. He took another deep breath and undid the diaper tabs. The stench hit him square in the face. He was going to throw up. No! He was a cowboy. He was stronger than this.

Mrs. Devers handed him another diaper. "Put this over his little wee-wee so he doesn't pee on you."

Phoenix did as instructed.

"Take the top of the diaper and wipe down under his wee-wee."

He did it quickly, trying not to breathe. She handed him a baby wipe, and he wiped Jake's bottom clean and whipped another diaper under him and had it secured in seconds. He felt like raising up his arms in victory. He hadn't thrown up. He'd done it.

The rest of the morning was a lesson in taking care of Jake, and Phoenix listened avidly. Soon Ms. Bauer arrived, and they left to go to the hearing to make Jake legally his. As he walked to the door, a strange feeling came over him, and he glanced back at Jake, who was playing with the little girl on the floor. He didn't want to leave his child. The parenting thing was settling in. He could do this. He could be a father.

He arrived at the hearing to learn that he had a lawyer. Rather, the deceased Mrs. Green had a lawyer and was handling Jake's case. The lawyer had a file he presented to the judge, which contained depositions from neighbors and people who knew Valerie. The judge asked Phoenix a few questions and then terminated Valerie's maternal rights, and Phoenix gained full custody. It didn't take long, but it seemed like a year had passed by the time he walked out of the courtroom.

They then went to the lawyer's office. Phoenix found out that Mrs. Green had a small savings account, and it had been put in trust for Jake's college education. He signed papers to become executor of the trust.

As Ms. Bauer drove them to Mrs. Green's house, she told him Valerie had almost bankrupted the old lady. The woman had to sell her home to pay off credit cards and loan sharks. She then rented a small house for herself, where Valerie stayed from time to time when she had nowhere else to go. But her grandmother absolutely refused to give her any more money.

The house was very neat, and everything was in its place. Jake's room was blue and white, and the bed was a warm honey color. Phoenix smiled at the sight. He almost took a picture to show Rosie. But Rosie would not be interested in seeing his son's room. A sad thought that chased the smile away.

Ms. Bauer brought a big box, and Phoenix put in a lot of toys and things he thought Jake would need, mostly clothes. Then he found Jake's baby book. He thumbed through it, eagerly watching his son grow in the arms of an elderly woman who clearly loved him. Tears stung the backs of his eyes. He put the album and other baby photos in the box and labeled it. They carried it to the post office to mail to Texas.

He had a flight out at five, so he had to hurry to get Jake and make it to the airport. Mrs. Devers had already packed Jake's few belongings. He thanked the Devers for taking such good care of Jake and then lifted Jake into his arms and walked out the door. He'd thought Jake would cry, but he didn't. After strapping Jake into the car seat in Ms. Bauer's car, they were off to the airport.

Jake did well on the flight, even though they were delayed an hour. Phoenix finally gave him the truck and trailer and horses. He didn't want to do that at the house because he didn't have anything for the other children. After the plane took off, the stewardess allowed Jake to play with the toy set in front of the seat because they had the front row and there was a little room. Soon Jake grew tired, and he crawled onto Phoenix's lap as if he had done it many times before.

Phoenix gathered him close. "We're going to Texas, son. To a big ranch with horses, cows…"

"Horse," Jake interrupted, holding up the toy in his hand.

"Yes, horse. You'll meet your uncles, aunts, cousins, grandpa and grandma."

"Ma Ma," Jake looked around the plane, and tears filled his eyes when he didn't see his great-grandmother. "Ma Ma."

"No, another grand—" He was afraid to say the rest of it. He didn't want to make Jake cry. "You see, I have a mother, and she will be another grandmother for you. Do you understand?"

Jake just stared at him with sad eyes. Of course he didn't understand. That was okay. In time he would. Phoenix felt sure of that.

Jake sat in his lap and played with the horses. A smile touched Phoenix's lips. Rosie was wrong. His kid liked horses. He would be just like Phoenix. He was going to enjoy telling her that.

He had a window seat and looked out at the fluffy clouds. He could walk on those clouds more easily than he could change Rosie's mind about him. Too much bad blood between the families. But he sure liked her. And he was going to introduce her to Jake just as soon as he could.

## Chapter Five

Rosie spent Sunday doing laundry. She'd installed a washer and dryer in the barn for convenience. One of these days, she would have a home with a washer and dryer in it. That was one of her goals for the future.

She then washed out the horse trailer and took care of the horses. She had two more mares that she rode occasionally, but Golden Lady was her favorite. When she was away from the circuit, she practiced and practiced because winning was her livelihood.

Soon she would have to look for another piece of land, which was too bad because she'd fallen in love with the tall oaks on this property, the quietness and the seclusion. Her closest neighbor was a mile away. Sometimes it was lonely and that's when she got out and worked around the place. Then she was too tired to care.

There were electricity and water on the property, and that was a big plus. When she was at home, she plugged into the electricity and didn't have to worry about the generator. She unrolled the awning over the door and had a table and chairs outside so it wasn't so crowded. With the winter months coming it would be hard to eat outside.

Through the weekend she couldn't get Phoenix Rebel out of her mind. She still couldn't believe she'd run into him.

She fixed iced tea and carried it outside to the table. Dixie jumped up onto her lap and she stroked the small dog. Since it was Monday, Phoenix should be home with his son, and she wondered how he was coping. She tried to force those thoughts away, but they kept intruding like bugs at a picnic.

There was just something about him that she couldn't ignore. Maybe it was his trigger-finger smile. Or maybe his never-give-up attitude. It was something and it was driving her crazy. She had to stop thinking about him.

She lived on a county road southeast of Temple, and it wasn't far from the McCray property. So many times she'd wanted to go home just to see if her father had forgiven her, but she always resisted the urge because she knew Ira McCray never forgave anyone. Ever.

She didn't know why she wanted to go home, because there was nothing there for her anymore. Her mother had passed away and her sister, Maribel, was nowhere to be found. Their father had kicked her out, because she'd gotten pregnant in high school, and Rosie was forbidden to have any contact with her. But now there was no man telling Rosie what she could or couldn't do. Some day she would find her sister.

Her brothers had their own lives and thought little of Rosie and her predicament. They never offered her any help when their father insisted she marry a man twice her age.

Dixie jumped off her lap to chase a squirrel, her favorite pastime. The place had lots of squirrels in the big oaks. They played in the yard and munched on the acorns and it drove Dixie crazy. Dixie got lots of exercise when they were home.

*Home.*

The word had a nice ring to it. But would she ever feel at home again?

IT WAS LATE when Phoenix drove into the yard at the bunkhouse. He'd called his mother and told her she would have to wait until Tuesday morning to meet Jake because he was asleep. She didn't like it. The family was coming at him from all sides. Quincy had called three times. Jude called. Paxton called. They all thought he couldn't handle being a father and wanted to help. For some reason he didn't want their help. He could do this alone.

He carried the diaper bag and Jake into the dark house, leaving the rest until morning. Quietly he made his way to his room and closed the door. Then he turned on the light. Jake was out, but he had to get him in his pajamas for the night. Changing a sleeping baby was an exercise in patience. It was like trying to dress a snake. Finally he had Jake tucked into the new baby bed. Jericho had set it up. Then he noticed a small chest of drawers in the corner and a trash can for diapers. His mother had been here. There was no doubt.

Phoenix sat on the bed, his elbows on his knees, his face in his hands. Was he doing the right thing? Could he take care of Jake? Could he be a good father? He was used to having fun and looking out for himself, and now Jake needed someone to be responsible for him. That was daunting to Phoenix, who never had much responsibility in his whole life.

He stood and brushed the hair from Jake's forehead. "We're in this together, son."

With that thought in mind, he stripped out of his

clothes and went to bed, ready to face the following day with family crowding in on him.

After breakfast the next morning, Phoenix got his overnight bag out of the truck. He'd stuffed some of Jake's clothes and toys inside. Their living quarters were going to be crowded from now on.

He gave Jake a bath and dressed him for the day in pull-up pants, a T-shirt and sneakers. He had to buy his son some jeans and soon. His son would wear jeans and boots.

Phoenix carried Jake into the living area to the toys he'd brought in. Paxton was on the sofa working on his bull rope. Jericho had left for work early.

"Watch Jake for a minute so I can take a shower."

Paxton looked at his nephew on the floor. "What?"

"Watch him, Pax. Don't let him out of your sight."

"We're in the living room. Where can he go?"

"Just watch him." Phoenix headed to the bathroom and showered and changed clothes as fast as he could. When he went into the living room, Paxton was still working on his bull rope and Jake wasn't there.

"Where's Jake?"

Paxton's head jerked up. "What? He was just here."

"Well, he's not here now." Phoenix noticed the front door was open and he ran for it, knowing Jake had found a way out. Damn! Outside, he looked both ways and saw Jake near the big barn, toddling as fast as he could go.

"Jake!" Phoenix shouted and ran to his son. He scooped him into his arms and held him tight and realized he was shaking. He'd only had his son a few hours, but the thought of losing him twisted his gut into a pretzel.

"Ma Ma," Jake said.

Phoenix patted Jake's back. "I understand, son." Phoenix didn't know how to make his son's pain better, and he hoped that in time Jake would forget. Not that he wanted him to forget his great-grandmother. He just wanted him to forget the pain of losing her.

Paxton caught up with them. "You found him."

"Yes. He could have gotten trampled by horses or cows or run over by a truck. Honestly, Paxton, sometimes you make me so mad."

"I'm sorry. I just took my eyes off him for a minute."

They walked toward the bunkhouse. "They told me that he's a runner," Phoenix said. "If he can get out a door, he will run, looking for his great-grandmother. I should've told you."

"I'm not watching him anymore. That's too much responsibility for this free-living cowboy."

"Watching a chicken is too much responsibility for you."

"Hey!"

He changed Jake's diaper, and then they were ready to go to the big house. He slung the strap of the diaper bag over his shoulder and knew in the next few weeks the bag would become his BFF. *Have bag. Can change diaper without throwing up.* He should have that stitched on it in bold letters.

Picking up his son, he said, "We're going to see your other grandmother."

Jake twisted his hands. "Dad-dy."

Looking at his son's precious face, he realized he'd forgotten to comb Jake's hair. He reached into the diaper bag and found the comb in the side pocket. With more skill than he'd thought he had, he combed his son's hair, only to have it fall right back in his eyes. He had to get it cut, and there was no way to do that before visiting with his mother.

Paxton followed them to the house, and as they went through the back door, he heard voices. Jude must be up. When he walked in, the room became very quiet.

"Oh, my, look at that baby." His mother came toward them with her hands outstretched. Jake turned away and buried his face in Phoenix's shoulder.

"He's a little shy. You'll have to give him time."

Jude got up and came toward them. "Your son is shy? He doesn't get that from you."

Elias and Grandpa were also at the table. A truck door slammed and soon his brother Egan, with his son Justin in a carrier, and his wife Rachel were in the room. Phoenix walked into the den to give Jake a little breathing space. And himself, too. Soon Quincy and Jenny came in, followed by Leah and Falcon and their year-and-half-old son, John.

Phoenix sat on the sofa with Jake in his lap. "You have to give him some time. He's a little nervous right now. I don't think he's ever been around this many people."

"We just want to see him," Quincy said. "We'll give him plenty of time to adjust."

John toddled over to them. Jake had a toy horse in his hand and he held it out to John saying, "Horse."

John took it and ran toward his mother. Jake immediately scrambled off Phoenix's lap and went after his horse. *Oh, no. Please don't hit John*, Phoenix silently prayed. He was on his feet to stop it.

Jake tried to pull the horse away from John, but John held on. Then he did exactly what he was doing at Mrs. Devers's. He hit John, and Leah came unglued.

"He hit my baby! Falcon, do something." She grabbed

her son and cuddled him as if he was a baby. Before Falcon could move, John pushed against his mother until she put him down again. He then ran to Jake, who took off and the two of them ran around the sofa, giggling. Once Jake stopped, John tackled him, and they rolled around on the floor, giggling that much more.

"What are they doing?" Leah asked.

"They're being little boys," Falcon told her. "That's what little boys do, and that's how they play."

"Well, I don't like it."

Falcon put an arm around his wife. "Honey, don't take this the wrong way, but you're making a momma's boy out of him."

At that moment, Jake finally saw the baby in the carrier Egan was holding. "Ba-by." He pointed and ran over to it.

Egan immediately raised the carrier higher, and that made Phoenix mad. He picked up his son and showed him the baby. "This is your cousin, Justin."

"Ba-by." He leaned over as if he wanted to kiss it.

"Do you want to kiss baby Justin?"

He leaned farther over, and Egan pushed the carrier closer. Jake kissed Justin's cheek. "Ba-by."

"He's not going to hurt him, Egan," Phoenix had to say for his own peace of mind. "He gets a little aggressive when something is taken from him, which I think only started when his great-grandmother passed away. I'm hoping it will change when he knows that I love him and I'm never leaving him."

"It was just a gut reaction."

Phoenix accepted the apology and knew it was time to leave. "Jake's had enough family for the morning."

His brothers said goodbye and filed out of the house, except Quincy and Jenny and Jude.

As Elias passed Phoenix, he threw an arm across Phoenix's shoulders. "You find a lot of ways to get out of work, but this is a brand-new one. But since it's such a good one, I'll do your work today."

Elias was always razzing him about getting all the easy jobs because he was their mother's favorite.

"Thanks."

Grandpa stopped and touched Jake's head. Phoenix was surprised his son didn't pull away. "I'm your great-grandpa. Can you say Grandpa?"

"Pa."

"Yep." Grandpa gave a crooked smile, and Phoenix hoped he wasn't going to spiral off into one of his long stories. "You and me are going to be good friends, and I'll tell you lots of stories about your daddy."

"Dad-dy."

"Come on, Grandpa," Elias called. "I'll take you back to your house before I go to work."

Grandpa winked at Jake. "I'll see you later, little whippersnapper."

Quincy and Jenny were the next to leave and, as always, Quincy had something to say. "Jenny and I were talking, and if you need someone to keep Jake while you're on the circuit, we'd be happy to."

"Jake stays with me. I'm not leaving him anywhere. He's been through enough and I wouldn't do that to him. Besides, Jenny is pregnant and needs to get as much rest as possible."

Quincy nodded. "Okay, but if you change your mind, just let us know."

"I told him that." Jenny kissed Jake's cheek. "But we're here if you need us."

Phoenix's patience was wearing thin like an old rope that had been used too many times. Before he walked out the door, though, he had to face his mother and another argument.

He turned to look at his mother's troubled brown eyes, and his resolve weakened. Falcon and Jude had raised their children in the house so their mother could help with them. But this was different. His family didn't think he could raise Jake alone. That's what bothered him.

"Jude got the baby bed out of the attic, and I put it up in my room," his mother was saying. "I just assumed Jake would stay with me while you're on the circuit. That's no place for a baby."

This was round three, and Phoenix had to get through it without wavering. "Like I told Quincy, Jake stays with me at all times. He needs to know that I'm not going to leave him. That's important to me. And to Jake."

"Son, babies adjust easily. Jake knows you're his father and that's not going to change, but you need to think of what's best for Jake."

"I am." He stood his ground. "I'm taking him back to the bunkhouse. Meeting so many people has been hard on him. It needs to be the two of us for a while."

"Are you saying you don't want me to see him?"

The old guilt trip was layered thick with hurt feelings, and Phoenix was having a hard time sticking to a decision he knew was right for him and Jake.

"No. You can come to the bunkhouse and see him anytime you want. But Jake has to learn that his home is with me."

"Phoenix, this is crazy. I can take care of that baby

and you can continue on with the rodeo circuit. It's very simple. I don't understand why you're making it so hard."

He gritted his teeth to keep words from spewing out. He would never be rude to his mother. But she looked at him like a young boy who couldn't handle responsibility. He wasn't that boy anymore. He'd changed the moment he'd found out he was a father.

"I'm doing what's best for Jake." He said the words slowly and firmly.

"It's not best to drag that kid all over the country, Phoenix. He needs a home."

"I realize that." He turned toward the door, not able to stand there and defend his decision one minute longer. "I'll see you later."

Jude followed him out. "Come on, Phoenix. Mom is just trying to help. Would leaving Jake here be so bad?"

Phoenix stopped and stared at his brother. "Would you leave Zane for days at a time?"

Jude looked down at the ground.

"No, you wouldn't, and I'm not leaving my son, either. That may be hard for everyone to understand, but it's my decision, so please stop pressuring me."

Jude held up his hands. "Okay, but please invite Mom over to visit with Jake."

He was starting to feel claustrophobic from all the family advice. He just wanted one of them to say he could raise Jake and be a responsible, mature adult. Just one of them. That's all he wanted. But now he would have to prove it.

"Zane is going to want to meet him, too. He's upstairs with his mother, finishing a paper for school this morning."

Jude, Paige and their thirteen-year-old son Zane lived

in the house with Mom, and that worked for them. But Phoenix knew it would never work for him.

"I'll make sure Zane meets his cousin."

"Thanks." Suddenly Jude reached out and hugged his brother and Jake. "I know you can do this. Please believe that. But we're all a little anxious for you."

Jude always knew the right thing to say. They were born in the same year and grew up like twins and were close. They were the two Rebel boys who'd been shot by Ezra McCray, and they shared a bond that could never be broken. Phoenix witnessed that today.

"Thanks. See you later." Phoenix walked toward the bunkhouse, holding his son. Every now and then Jake would hold the toy horse up and say, "Horse."

As Phoenix walked, he had to admit he also was a little nervous about caring for Jake. He didn't want to do the wrong thing for his son. What he needed was a woman's touch, and Rosie McCray's face snapped into his mind with vivid clarity. It was a little crazy and disorienting, but it felt right and good like gravy on mashed potatoes.

"How does the name Rosie sound to you, son?"

"Horse."

"My thoughts exactly."

## Chapter Six

Phoenix loaded Jake into his car seat and drove into town to the grocery store. He had to buy food for his son. Mrs. Devers had given him a list and he followed it—up to a point. He added SpaghettiOs because he had liked SpaghettiOs as a kid and he felt that Jake would like them, too. They were on the menu for lunch.

While Jake played with his toys in the living room, Phoenix put up the groceries. He was about to open a can of SpaghettiOs when his mother walked in.

"Hi, son." She placed a basket covered with a red-checked cloth on the counter. "I made fried chicken, green beans and mashed potatoes and gravy and brought some for you and Jake. I'm on my way to carry lunch to your brothers."

Phoenix sighed inwardly. His mother just wasn't going to let up. She didn't trust him to raise Jake. That hurt.

She went over to the sofa and sat down, watching Jake play. She reached down, picked him up and placed him on her lap. Jake didn't resist. He just stared at her with big eyes.

"You look just like your daddy."

"Dad-dy." Jake pointed to him.

"It's uncanny how he knows that," his mother said.

"Yeah, isn't it?" He couldn't hide the sarcasm in his voice, and he wasn't sure he wanted to.

"How are you doing changing diapers?" she asked. "I worry about your weak stomach."

He clenched his jaw. "I'm handling it." He wouldn't tell her he had to hold his breath and he almost threw up his breakfast this morning.

"You know, I could do that. I don't have a problem changing diapers."

"Mom, I know you're trying to help, but Jake needs me right now. Not his grandmother or his uncles or his aunts. He needs me."

"I never realized you were so stubborn."

He hadn't, either. He was usually easygoing and willing to pass off responsibility in the blink of an eye. But not this time.

She kissed Jake's cheek. "Grandma has to go. Your uncles are waiting for lunch, but I'll see you soon." She placed Jake on the floor and walked out.

"Ma." Jake got to his feet and ran for the door, but Phoenix beat him to it. He picked him up and stared into his watery eyes.

"It's okay, son. It's time for lunch."

"Ba-ba, Dad-dy."

That's what Jake called his bottle. Phoenix thought this might be a good time to wean him. He reached for a small glass in the cabinet and put some milk in it. When he tried to get Jake to drink from it, the kid shook his head and shouted, "No!"

"Daddy wants you to drink out of the glass."

Jake's face scrunched into a frown. "No."

Phoenix gave up. It might be too soon.

While Jake took a nap, Phoenix put a latch on the door so Jake couldn't get out. Then he sat on the sofa and went to sleep. Taking care of a child was hard work. He'd never realized that before.

In the afternoon, Leah, John and Grandpa came over, with Leah pulling John in a red wagon. Jake and John crawled in and out of it, giggling and playing, having the time of their lives. Leah apologized for overreacting earlier that morning. Phoenix really didn't have any bad feelings about it. Kids were kids.

Then Paige and Zane came over to meet Jake, and it was another round of meeting people. But Jake adjusted well. Tomorrow, Phoenix decided, he would have to do something different. Family wasn't going to leave them alone. He didn't know why that was so important to him, but he felt he and Jake needed this time alone to bond.

That night his mother sent pot roast for supper by way of Paxton. Phoenix knew he wasn't going to win this battle, but he was determined to make changes. Rico came in from work and they ate. Once again, Phoenix tried to get Jake to drink out of a glass, but he refused loudly. After that, Phoenix gave Jake a bath and got him ready for bed.

Jake ran into the living area in his SpongeBob SquarePants pajamas. Rico was in his recliner, watching television, and Paxton was sprawled on the sofa, drinking beer.

Jake went over to him, pointing to the beer bottle. "Mmm. Mmm. Mmm."

"He wants beer, Phoenix."

"Don't give him any." As he said the words, a thought occurred to him. He went over to Paxton and took the bottle out of his hand.

"Hey."

"I'll bring you another."

He looked at Jake. "You want beer?"

"Mmm. Mmm. Mmm." Jake reached for the bottle.

"Stay with Uncle Paxton and I'll get you some."

"What are you doing?" Paxton called.

"Being sneaky. I've been trying to get him to drink out of a glass, but he won't." He quickly poured the beer down the drain, reached for the milk in the refrigerator and filled the bottle about half-full. Carrying it back into the living room, he said, "Come here, Jake. Daddy'll give you some beer."

Jake crawled onto his lap, and Phoenix held the beer bottle so Jake could sip it. He didn't have time to rinse out the bottle, so it had to have some beer taste in it. But he didn't worry about that as he held his breath.

Jake took a sip, then another sip and then another. In Phoenix's arms, he continued to drink from the bottle. It wasn't ideal but, at least, Jake wasn't sucking on a nipple. Soon Phoenix would have him drinking from a glass. That was his plan.

"Now I've seen everything," Rico said.

"Where's my beer?" Paxton asked.

Cradling Jake to him, Phoenix got up, went to the refrigerator, got Paxton another beer and threw it to him from across the room.

"Damn, Phoenix. Now it's going to spew all over me."

"It's like living in a zoo," Rico said with a smile.

"He's out. I'm putting Jake to bed."

"'Night, little fella," Rico said. Because of the scar and the long hair, most kids were scared of Rico, but Jake had taken to him like a duck took to water.

Phoenix put Jake to bed and he crashed, too.

THE NEXT MORNING Phoenix plucked a beer out of the refrigerator and handed it to Paxton, who was sitting at the table eating.

"Drink this."

Paxton raised his head and glared at him. "What? You want me to drink beer for breakfast? I have to work today."

"I want to put Jake's milk in it. Maybe he'll drink it that way without using his baby bottle."

Paxton laid down his fork. "You do realize how stupid this sounds?"

"I didn't ask for advice. Do you want the beer or not? I'm pouring it down the drain."

Paxton grabbed the bottle. "Your kid is going to drink out of a beer bottle and I'm going to become an alcoholic."

"We'll adjust."

"Yeah, right."

Phoenix poured the beer into a glass. All the time Paxton was shaking his head. Phoenix knew this was a little crazy, but then, his whole life was crazy. He poured milk into the bottle and set it in the refrigerator.

"Jake, breakfast," he called, and Jake came running.

Phoenix lifted him into the high chair and placed his breakfast in front of him. Jake ate the eggs and sausage with his fingers.

"Ba-ba, Dad-dy."

Phoenix reached into the refrigerator for the bottle. "You want some beer?"

"Beer." Jake wiggled his feet excitedly. This time Jake took big gulps and was drinking the milk really well from the bottle. At Jake's eagerness to drink from the bottle, Phoenix had to wonder if Mrs. Green drank beer. It seemed to be something Jake recognized. The picture he had of the little old lady just didn't jibe with her drinking beer.

"That's going to get you into so much trouble," Paxton said as he got up from the table and reached for his hat. "I'm going to work before you warp my mind, and if I were you I'd hide that beer bottle before Mom comes over."

Rico grabbed his hat, too, and ruffled Jake's hair. "Bye, little fella." Then he frowned at Paxton. "I can smell beer on you. You'd better drink another cup of coffee."

"Damn, Phoenix. Now you're going to get *me* in trouble."

Phoenix smiled as they went out the door. He knew it was pretty bad having his kid drink from a beer bottle, but maybe he could wean him to a glass in a couple of days. Oh, man. This wasn't the way to raise a kid. He was almost positive of that.

Ms. HENSHAW PAID a surprise visit to finalize the custody in Texas. She was not happy Phoenix lived in the bunkhouse, but he explained he was a working cowboy and his kid lived where he did. After checking where Jake would sleep and making sure he had everything he needed, she signed off on the custody and wished him well.

Later, he packed the diaper bag and a cooler with milk. He needed three empty beer bottles. He poured the contents down the drain and said, "Lord, forgive me." In cowboy church, that had to be a sin.

As he was driving out, he called his mother. "Mom, I'm taking Jake into town to get a haircut and then I'm going to buy him some clothes, so there's no need for you to worry about lunch or supper. Just concentrate on the roundup."

"I was hoping you'd let me keep Jake today and you could help with the roundup."

He tightened his grip on the steering wheel, fighting for the right to be a father to his kid in the way he wanted. That way might not be the right way, but he was doing the best he could, even if he had empty beer bottles in his cooler.

"I don't think Jake will be comfortable with anyone else right now. I probably won't be able to help much with the roundup until I have Jake settled. I'm willing to add more of my earnings to the Rebel Ranch account."

"You know you don't have to do that. I'll take care of it. Just take care of your son."

From the beginning he and Paxton had made a deal with their brothers: they would give half of their winnings to the ranch in return for them not being there to help. It had worked well, especially since they started winning. So Phoenix didn't harbor any guilty feelings about that. He just had this big ache in his stomach from his mother treating him like he was fifteen years old.

At that moment he was never more aware of his mother's favoritism. He was the baby and she always took his side when he had a riff with the brothers, like the time he spiked the punch at a party and got Grandpa, Eden and Zane sick. Falcon and Jude were gunning for him. But his mother smoothed it over as if nothing bad had happened. Falcon should have beaten him to a pulp. Phoenix would have been very upset if someone had done that to Jake. Suddenly, being the favorite was not a good feeling.

Phoenix took Jake to the local barbershop that was run by two old cowboys who told stories just as vivid and untrue as Grandpa's. Jake sat very still in the chair and kept his eyes on Phoenix as if to make sure he wasn't leaving.

Afterward Phoenix asked Jake, "Ready to go shopping for jeans and boots?"

"Boots," Jake said as Phoenix strapped him into the car seat.

He ran around to the driver's side and paused before backing out of his spot. What he needed was some help. A woman's help. A blue-eyed redhead's help. But how did he find her? Especially when she didn't want to see him.

He pulled out his phone. She might have a Facebook page like most rodeo riders. Zane had set one up for Phoenix and Paxton. He clicked onto his Facebook page and typed in Rosie's name in the search. Her page came up immediately, and there she was with her long hair and tight jeans on that beautiful palomino. But the horse paled into insignificance compared with the rider. The page said she lived in Temple, Texas. That could be anywhere in the area. How did he find her address? The sensible part of his brain seemed to have stopped working.

A picture of her live-in trailer parked to the left of a red barn caught his eye. There was something on the barn. He made the picture larger and centered it on the barn. It was numbers, one on the left and one on the right. Could they be part of her address? Maybe a county road?

"Dad-dy."

"Daddy's playing investigator, Jake."

"Horse." Jake held up the toy in his hand.

"Yeah, horse." He looked back at his son. At night Jake slept with Floppy, the dog, but the horse was the first thing he picked up every morning. Somehow the horse connected Jake to him.

He glanced at the barn again. The right number had to be a Bell County road, and the number on the left had to be the address. So he used his GPS and typed in the address. It worked like a charm.

"What do you think, Jake? Should we go shopping by ourselves or enlist the aid of a pretty woman?"

"Horse."

He knew what he was going to do. He didn't feel good about it, but he was desperate. Jake was his kid and if he let go just for an instant, his family would take over. Phoenix was Jake's father and the one who took care of him. He was holding on with all his might to keep his son with him. It was a little daunting to realize how much power his mother wielded over him.

With the GPS in his truck he found the county road easily and then just watched the numbers on the mailboxes. There weren't that many. The houses were few and far between. He passed her home before he realized he'd reached it. While he turned around, he thought about what he was doing: making friends with the enemy. The Rebel/McCray feud blasted to the forefront of his mind.

The feud had destroyed and eventually killed their father, and his mother had grieved for him since. Phoenix saw it every day in his mother's eyes. So what was he doing here? As he maneuvered the truck, some of his dad's words came back to him: *Whenever you have a problem that seems insurmountable, just lead with your heart, son, and you'll be fine.*

*I'm leading with my heart, Dad.*

He felt his dad would understand.

He stopped at Rosie's entrance and stared at the property. The trailer was there and her truck was parked near the small barn. And that's all there was. He didn't see a house. Maybe it was farther back in the woods. He drove over the cattle guard, refusing to think about what he was doing—invading her privacy. Maybe he was a wild Rebel after all.

Rosie had spent the morning working with the horses. She had a rodeo in Stephenville on Friday and she didn't want Lady getting stiff or lax. She barrel-raced all three of her horses just to keep them in shape. The barrels were set up in the corral and she tried to race them often. Of course, while she was away the other two horses got time off, but sometimes she carried an extra with her. But they couldn't keep up with Lady's speed.

After taking care of the horses and feeding them, she went back to the trailer. Between the trailer and the barn she had an old water trough and had filled it with water, letting the sunshine warm it. She had only a shower in the trailer, and she loved taking a bath.

She stripped out of her clothes and laid them on a chair she'd put beside the trough. After pinning up her hair, she slid into the water and gasped. Goose bumps popped up on her skin from the coolness, but soon she adjusted to it. She sprinkled bubble bath in and reached for the scented soap and scrubbed away the grime from the morning. Then she just relaxed, floating around in the water. There was nothing like a bath.

Her tranquility was interrupted by a sound. Dixie barked and Rosie sat up. It sounded like a truck crossing the cattle guard. She listened closely. Yes, that's what it was. It could be the Tisdales from down the road. Sometimes Mrs. Tisdale baked and brought Rosie a treat. But she usually called. And Rosie had had her phone with her at all times.

Who could it be?

She quickly stepped out of the trough and dried her body. Pulling on her panties and jeans, she groaned. It wasn't an easy task when her body was damp. She didn't even bother with her bra. She just pulled a T-shirt over her head.

This was a secluded area, and she usually wasn't worried about bathing between the trailer and the barn because there was no one around. But today apprehension skittered across her nerves.

She left her boots by the trough and tiptoed around the trailer to see who had invaded her privacy. Her heart raced and anger shot through her like a thousand stinging ants. Phoenix Rebel was getting a child out of a car seat. How had he found her? How dare he!

Living out here alone, she had a gun to protect herself, but it was in the trailer. She'd never had any cause to use it. It was more of a security measure. But she wished she had it now.

She marched over to his truck, ready to tear into him like a wild hyena. But he turned with the little boy in his arms. The boy had short, dark hair and big brown eyes and the most precious face she'd ever seen. All her anger floated away like bubbles in the bath.

For a moment.

How dare he do this to her!

She forced her attention to Phoenix's face and braced herself against the attraction she saw there. He truly had to have been created when God was in a good mood. His chiseled features were perfectly etched, showcasing warm, dark eyes and a mouth that was molded for laughter and fun. The curve of it spoke volumes. It was a kissable mouth. A touchable, kissable... Oh, heavens. She was in so much trouble. She had to make a stand now.

"Please leave. I did not invite you here, nor do I want to see you. I thought you understood that."

"Okay. You have a right to be angry. I just wanted you

to meet Jake. I know that sounds crazy, and I might be a little crazy. I'm told that a lot."

She took a deep breath. "How did you find me?"

"If you'll stop being angry for a minute, I'll explain. By the way, this is Jake."

She refused to look at the little boy. She couldn't. If she did, she would be lost. Phoenix knew that. That's why he'd brought his son out here. She couldn't get involved with Phoenix or his child and she had to make that clear.

"Please go away and don't come back." She marched to the door of the trailer and went inside without a backward glance. But she'd forgotten one thing: Dixie. She was barking agitatedly. If she was by the door, Rosie could just let her in. The sound was coming from farther out in the yard. She was barking at Phoenix and his son. Dixie loved kids, and she was probably trying to get the boy to play with her.

Oh no.

What could she do now?

## Chapter Seven

"Jake. Come back here. Jake!"

Rosie listened at the door, and all she could hear was Phoenix's voice. Dixie had stopped barking and that bothered her. The dog was always excited around children. There was only one thing to do. She had to face this like an adult instead of hiding in the trailer like a scared little girl.

Gently she eased the door open and peeped outside. She saw no one. They weren't in the front yard. As she stepped outside, she could hear Phoenix calling, "Jake, come out of there."

On the other side of the trailer, she found Phoenix squatting and looking under it.

"What's going on?"

He turned to look at her. "Your dog ran under the trailer, and Jake followed before I could stop him. Now I can't get him out."

Rosie knelt in the grass, near the trough she'd been bathing in, and looked under the trailer. "Come here, Dixie. Come to me."

The dog trotted out without a problem and went to Rosie, licking her face. Rosie scooped her up and held her close.

"Come on, Jake," Phoenix called. "Come to Daddy."

The boy began to cry. Loud wails echoed from beneath the trailer.

"Hey, son. Don't cry. Daddy's right here. Just come out from there."

But the wails grew louder.

Phoenix lay flat on his stomach and crawled under the trailer to get his son. In a few seconds, he scooted out with the boy in his arms. Phoenix sat on the grass and cuddled him. "It's okay. You're out. See? Look around."

"'Cared."

Phoenix patted the little boy's back. "It's okay, son." After a few moments the little boy stopped crying. He raised his head from Phoenix's shoulder, tears glistening in his beautiful eyes. His father's eyes. There was no doubt this boy was Phoenix's son.

"Beer, Dad-dy."

Rose's mouth fell open and she closed it quickly. "You're giving him beer?"

"Now, don't get your feathers ruffled. I can explain."

"I can't think of a way you can justify that."

He kissed the boy's cheek and Rosie thought how good he was with the baby. He was a natural father and the boy responded to him. "Play with Dixie and I'll go get it."

Jake toddled over and Dixie shot away. The boy followed, giggling, and then they were playing, rolling in the grass. Rosie was mesmerized by the sight. What a gift a child was.

Before she knew it, Phoenix was back, kneeling just a little too close for her comfort. He opened a cooler and poured milk into an empty beer bottle.

"You've got to be kidding."

"The foster mother told me Jake needs to be weaned

from a bottle, but he won't drink out of a glass. I tried and he refused. Paxton was drinking a beer and Jake wanted it. So I poured the beer out and put milk in it and it worked like a charm."

"So your plan now is to give your son milk out of a beer bottle?"

"Until I can get him to drink out of a glass. He didn't even ask for his bottle last night."

"Cowboy, have you ever heard of a sippy cup?"

His eyes glowed like embers. Once again she couldn't look away, and she hated herself for that weakness. "Oh, I think my nephew John has one of those."

"Yes. Doesn't your family help you with him?"

Jake dropped into his lap, reaching for the beer bottle. Phoenix sat in the grass, cradled the boy in his arms and let him drink. It was only for a few seconds and then Jake shot away again, chasing Dixie.

Closing the cooler, Phoenix said, "Family is my problem."

"How?" She sat cross-legged, waiting for him to explain.

He leaned back, using his hands for support, his long legs outstretched in front of him. "You see, I'm not known for responsibility or maturity. Sad but true."

"I can believe that."

"Hey!"

"Well, you turn up here uninvited. That's immature and irresponsible."

His sun browned skin faded a little. "Okay, that was out of line, but I was desperate." He crossed his boots at the ankles, and she stared at the long length of cowboy. She didn't understand why she was so aware of him. She was around cowboys all the time, and they teased and flirted and acted crazy. That was typical. She was used to it. But something about Phoenix just pushed her buttons.

"My mother wants me to move into the house. She has a baby bed set up and everything is ready. All I have to do is give in and she'll raise my son. Quincy and Jude, two of my brothers, have said they'd be willing to take Jake and care for him, especially when I'm on the circuit. They don't trust me to be a father. They don't trust me to take care of him like a father should."

She heard the hurt in his voice and wanted to reach out and hug him, which surprised her. She wasn't a hugging person. But she wanted him to feel better. That surprised her, too. "What I saw you doing a few minutes ago was very good. You've bonded with your son in a very short amount of time."

"He's my son and I intend to raise him. I intend for him to know that I'm his father and I will never leave him with anyone."

She pointed to his broad chest. "I think maturity and responsibility are taking root."

He leaned forward, that glow back in his eyes. "Then can I tempt you into going shopping with us? I need to buy Jake some jeans, boots and cowboy stuff. I'm hopeless in the baby department. You were so good at helping me in Walmart, and I thought I'd ask you again."

"Is that why you came here?"

He grinned. "Yes, ma'am."

"How did you find me?"

The grin broadened. "As easy as Facebook."

"My address is not on Facebook."

He pointed to the barn and the numbers she'd painted there for the truck driver who delivered feed for her horses.

"They're just numbers."

"And they're on a photo on your Facebook page. I enlarged it on my phone, and I could see the numbers clearer. I figured it was a county road number and address. With a little more searching I found it."

She ran her hands up her arms, feeling a little spooked. But oddly not from Phoenix. He was harmless. Now, that was the biggest understatement she'd ever thought. He was not harmless in so many other ways that involved her heart.

"I'll definitely take the picture off. I don't want strangers knowing where I live."

"Aw, no one's as smart as me, or as desperate."

"You're full of it."

"Yes, ma'am." His eyes traveled over her T-shirt and she realized it was damp, and without a bra her breasts were defined more than she wanted.

"Stop it."

His eyes traveled to face. "What?"

"Being a typical cowboy with your brains below your belt."

"Ah, c'mon."

She lifted an eyebrow and he shrugged. "Okay, I'm out of line again. But I don't think you realize just how beautiful and sexy you are, especially with those freckles across the bridge of your nose."

"Another cowboy line. Really? I've heard them all."

"I'm not going to win with you, am I?"

"No, so I'd just as soon you'd be honest instead of sleazy."

He looked over his shoulder. "Is your house back in the woods?"

A tingle of fear edged along her spine. She didn't want

to discuss her living arrangements. She didn't want to discuss anything with him. But she'd asked him to be honest so she had to be, too. Maybe then he would go away and never come back.

"No."

He glanced at the galvanized trough and the chair with her towel and toiletries. "You were taking a bath out here?"

"Yes, until you invaded my privacy." She wasn't embarrassed about her living arrangements. "I live in my trailer."

"Full-time. I mean…" Clearly he was stunned and unable to hide it.

"Yes. I'm on the road a lot, and for now it suits me."

Jake plopped into Phoenix's lap, out of breath from playing with Dixie. He held his son close, his eyes on her. "I'm not the gossipy type, but I've heard tidbits about you around the circuit, and the news is that you divorced a very rich man. Didn't you get something out of the divorce?"

"I got my freedom," she stated in a proud tone. "And that was worth more than anything money could buy." She wasn't going to talk about this anymore. She barely knew Phoenix, and sharing wasn't easy for her. It had been a horrible time in her life. Most days she could wipe it from her mind, but there were times late at night when the horror invaded her peaceful dreams. She shared that with no one.

"I can see you're uncomfortable with the subject," he said in a soothing tone, and that threw her. She never imagined a Rebel as consoling. She'd heard otherwise.

He turned his attention to his son. "Jake, ask Rosie if she'd like to go shopping with us."

*Nothing like a little blackmail.*

"Ro-sie," Jake said, and Rosie refused to look at the boy. At the baby voice, her heart swelled as if someone had pumped air into it. Any minute it was going to burst and flood her body with warm emotions she didn't know how to handle.

"Tell her we're sorry for invading her privacy."

"Sor-ry."

Unable to stop herself, she looked into the baby's eyes and saw everything that was missing in her life: the joy of a child. A lump the size of the Alamo formed in her throat. She couldn't cry. It would open up too many emotions, but she felt a crack in the solid steel armor she wore to keep herself safe from the pain. How had Phoenix Rebel gotten past all the security measures she had taken over the years to protect herself?

Dixie dropped one of Jake's sneakers into Rose's lap. She realized Jake's sneakers were missing from his feet and his socks were coated with dried grass.

With his back against his father's chest, Jake pointed at his shoe. "Mine."

"Is this yours?" She held up the sneaker.

Jake nodded.

"I wonder where the other one is." Phoenix looked around and then zeroed in on the trailer. "It's probably under there."

"Go get Jake's sneaker," Rosie said to Dixie. The dog shot under the trailer and came out with it.

"Now if I could get Jake to mind like that." Phoenix brushed the grass from his son's socks and put on his sneakers. With one fluid movement, he picked up his hat, placed it on his head and got to his feet with Jake in his arms. Jake rested his head on Phoenix's shoulder, closing his eyes.

"No, son. You can't go to sleep. You haven't had your lunch yet."

Rosie pushed to her feet. "You are hopeless, you know. You should have him on a schedule."

"I'm working on it." He walked toward his truck. "I'm really sorry I bothered you."

Suddenly all the energy and life he'd brought with him seemed to dim, and she felt lonelier than she ever had. Something good was within her reach and all she had to do was…

"Phoenix—"

He turned, a smile as wide as Texas on his face. "The lady knows my name."

She ignored the quakes of delight running through her. "I'll find something for Jake to eat, because he's going to fall asleep in the truck."

"We accept." He tickled Jake's stomach. "Don't we, son?"

"Just give me a few minutes to do a couple of things."

"Okay."

She ran to the trough and put the end of a long hose in it. She sucked on the other end until water came through and let it run out into the pasture. Taking a deep breath, she grabbed her towel and toiletries and ran into the house to change clothes and put on her bra.

Phoenix and Jake came into the trailer. Suddenly it was too small, too closed up, because she was very aware of Phoenix standing next to her. A woodsy scent mixed with baby powder tickled her nostrils and she wanted to laugh. She was accepting another person into her life, and that warmed and scared her at the same time. Since her divorce, she had avoided this because it brought too much pain. But now, with two sets of dark eyes staring at her, she made the biggest decision of her life because she could do nothing less.

They'd touched her heart. Somehow, just maybe, they needed her as much as she needed them.


PHOENIX SAT ON the small sofa at the end of the trailer with Jake on his lap. The trailer was bigger and nicer than the camper he and Paxton used. Neat and organized, too. Something he and Paxton knew nothing about.

There was a blue booth with a table and a small kitchen combined with the living space. A bedroom and bath were at the other end. He couldn't believe she lived here. It was nice to have a full trailer on the road, but he was always glad to get home to more space. So many questions plagued his mind about her, but he would keep them to himself for now. He was just happy she wasn't mad at him anymore.

He couldn't take his eyes off her as she worked in the small space. She was completely dressed now in jeans, boots and Western shirt. He rather liked the barefooted, wet T-shirt look. He liked everything about her. Her stubbornness, her fight for independence, her feistiness and something else he couldn't describe. Something deep inside drew him to her. Maybe it was the loneliness in her. Although he'd never been lonely. There were always family and friends around. But there was something about her that he couldn't look away from, nor did he want to.

She had food on the table in a few minutes, and he carried Jake to the booth. With no high chair, he had to hold him. His son reached for a piece of cut-up apple on a plate and munched on it.

"I guess he's hungry."

"I made macaroni and cheese. Kids love it."

He guessed he should've asked if he could help her, but his mother never let him in the kitchen except to do dishes. And he hated that. Now he had to step up and do more because he had a son.

Jake crawled out of his lap and over to Rosie, holding up his arms.

Rosie looked at Phoenix with panic in her eyes. "What does he want?"

"He wants you to pick him up." Had she never been around children? Her brothers Gunnar and Malachi had children, and she had to have been around them when she was younger. Maybe the fear in her eyes was about something else.

She carefully lifted Jake onto her lap. "He weighs hardly anything." Jake pointed to the mac and cheese. "Oh, okay." She spooned the food into his mouth, and Jake ate hungrily.

Phoenix picked up the grilled cheese sandwich in front of him, eating and watching Rosie with his son. A look of total entrancement was on her face, serene and relaxed. He had a feeling she didn't let herself relax very often, but Jake was working his magic.

"Ma Ma," Jake said, his bottom lip trembling. Phoenix put his sandwich down, not knowing what to do. There was no reason for Jake to think of his great-grandmother unless…his great-grandmother made mac and cheese for him.

"What's wrong?" Rosie asked. "Why is he upset? Did I do something wrong?"

"No." Phoenix got up and squatted in front of Rosie and Jake. "It's okay, son. Daddy's here."

They went back to eating and nothing else was said. Rosie even got Jake to drink milk out of a glass. She had a way with him. That was easy to see. Jake's eyelids began to droop, and Rosie laid him on the sofa and covered him with a blanket. Dixie jumped up and made herself comfortable beside him.

Phoenix sat on one end of the sofa and Rosie on the other. There weren't many places to sit in the trailer except for a comfy chair next to the sofa.

"What was that about?" Rosie asked.

He told her about Jake's great-grandmother and how much Jake missed her. "Obviously she must've made him macaroni and cheese."

"That's so sad. You have to tell him his great-grandmother is dead."

"Oh no, I can't do that. It will break his little heart. I'm just feeling my way right now and not equipped to handle something like that."

She shook her head, almost in disgust. "Who would you like to tell him such a thing?"

"I don't know. He's two years old and I'm hoping he'll just forget it."

Rosie's blue eyes stared steadily at him, and he wanted to squirm. He could do a lot of things, but the sad emotional stuff he knew he wasn't able to do. Most of the adults in his family took on that role. He was left with the easy stuff. That was a hell of an explanation and he didn't even buy it himself.

"Okay, I'm being a jerk."

"A scared jerk. Just tell him and maybe some of the sadness and the grief will leave his heart."

"I think you bring out the best in me."

She straightened the blanket over Jake. "I hardly know you."

"But we connect. I feel it and I know you feel it."

"Phoenix…"

"Okay. We don't need another problem here. I'll tell him when he wakes up, and you'd better be here to comfort both of us."

A smile touched the curve of her mouth and he was mesmerized.

FORTY-FIVE MINUTES LATER, Phoenix sat on the sofa with Jake on his lap, sipping milk out of a beer bottle. Phoenix had tried a glass first, but once again Jake refused loudly. After Jake was through, Phoenix took the bottle and handed it to Rosie. She lifted an eyebrow, urging him on.

He placed his hand on Jake's small chest and it covered the whole area. He could feel Jake's heartbeat thumping against his palm. "Son, Daddy wants to talk about… Ma Ma."

"Ma Ma." Jake looked around.

"No, Ma Ma's not here." He took a moment and prayed for the right words. Words that would not hurt his son. "Son, Ma Ma has gone to heaven to be with Jesus."

"Jes-us."

He was surprised when Jake said the word, but he remembered the CPS lady telling him that Mrs. Green took Jake to church. He knew the word and Phoenix hoped he knew a whole lot more, even at his young age. "Yes, Ma Ma is with Jesus and you're with Daddy. I'll always be here for you. Do you understand that?"

"Ma Ma."

Phoenix took a deep breath. "Ma Ma is gone. Jake is with Daddy."

Jake turned in the circle of Phoenix's arms and rested his face against Phoenix's chest. That's when the sobs came. Phoenix felt them all the way to his soul. In some ways Jake understood, and Phoenix just held him and let him cry for his great-grandmother.

Rosie sat beside him and put her arms around both of them. It was a bonding moment, and Phoenix wanted to stay in the circle of her gentle embrace because he knew with Rosie he had found a soft place to fall.

# Chapter Eight

Several times during the afternoon, Rosie told herself it was crazy for her to be out with Phoenix and his son. She was a McCray and he was a Rebel and they shouldn't even be speaking to each other. But when Phoenix looked at her with those deep, dark eyes, she forgot who she was. The only thing that registered was the way he made her feel: warm, excited and all woman.

He was so gentle with Jake. When he told the boy about his great-grandmother, all her defenses weakened. She didn't even think twice about going shopping with him. Little Jake hooked her right from the start, and it was very clear Phoenix needed help. They went to Walmart first and bought the sippy cup. Jake wasn't having anything to do with it until they found a SpongeBob one. He was all smiles then and wouldn't let it go. They bought other things she thought Phoenix would need. From there they went to a Western wear store.

Phoenix bought boots, jeans, shirts and a hat for Jake. The boy was very good about trying on clothes, except there was one problem. The jeans kept falling down. They had to buy a belt, and Jake shook his head at every one the salesclerk brought out.

Phoenix squatted in front of his son. "You have to have a belt to hold up your jeans."

"No!" Jake shouted. It was the first time he'd misbehaved all afternoon, and she could see Phoenix was at his wit's end about what to do.

She squatted by Jake. "What's the matter? Don't you like belts?"

"No! Dad-dy."

She couldn't make sense of that and neither could Phoenix. "Okay. Tell us what you want."

He pointed to Phoenix's belt.

"Yes, Daddy wears a belt, too."

"No!" Jake shouted again.

Rosie glanced at Phoenix. "Your turn."

"Son, show Daddy what you want."

Jake leaned over and pointed to Phoenix's buckle, and then it dawned on both of them. Jake wanted a buckle on his belt like his dad, but he didn't know what to call it.

She and Phoenix shared a secret smile as the salesclerk brought a buckle and put it on Jake's belt and then looped the belt around his pants. Jake was all smiles again, except when Phoenix tried to take the clothes off him. He threw a fit and cried loudly in the store.

"Okay, you can wear them." Phoenix gave in.

"The jeans really need to be washed," the salesclerk said.

"Don't worry," Phoenix told her. "They'll be wet in no time."

Jake walked out of the store between them, staring down at his boots. He tripped three times but refused to let Phoenix carry him. Once Phoenix put him in the car seat, Jake continued to stare at his boots.

"I think he loves the boots," Rosie said as they drove away.

"Yeah. That's my kid."

"I'm amazed that you're so good with him."

"I am, too." He laughed. "I have to admit I didn't know how this was going to go or how I was going to raise a kid, but I have a handle on it now and I can do this. I know I can do this." He glanced at her with a twinkle in his eyes. "With your help."

"You know it's crazy us being together."

"Yeah, I've always been a little crazy."

"I know that for a fact."

"Hey!"

She laughed, and it almost felt alien to her since it had been so long. A life without laughter was like a life without sunshine. And that described where she'd been emotionally—locked up in a dark existence without any light or warmth. Thanks to a dark-eyed man, she'd stepped out of the boundaries of the past and enjoyed the sunshine on her face and skin, breathed in the fresh air not tinged with grief or sadness, and welcomed the joy singing through her veins.

"I'm buying dinner. You choose the place."

She didn't even bother with a refusal, which would've been her way of staying to herself. Tonight, she didn't want to be alone.

They ate at Olive Garden, and she was enthralled as she watched Phoenix cut up Jake's spaghetti. Jake loved it and got spaghetti on his cheeks, his fingers and all over the high chair. Reaching out with his hand, Jake touched Phoenix's cheek and left spaghetti marks. Rosie had the urge to lean over the table and lick the sauce from Phoenix's roughened male skin. She'd never had urges like that before, and the feelings stunned and excited her at the same time. Phoenix Rebel was just irresistible, especially with his son. Or maybe all her hormones were kicking in—finally.

They arrived back at the trailer a little before six, and Rosie invited them in because it would be so lonely without them. That was a sad truth she hated to admit. But she was clinging to this time as long as she could. She couldn't explain it to herself so she just went with the moment.

Jake immediately started playing with Dixie, chasing her around the trailer. Phoenix sat on the sofa.

"Would you like some coffee?"

"No, thanks. I have to go pretty soon. My family's probably wondering what happened to me."

"Do you always stay in contact?"

"Nah. But my mom is a little antsy about Jake."

"You're doing a great…" Jake was trying to crawl to Dixie and having a hard time in his boots. He'd lost one and was dragging the other on the linoleum. "Wait a minute, Jake." She squatted and removed his other boot and placed both of them on the table.

"You're very good with kids," he remarked.

"I guess I was about nine when my brother Gunnar's first son was born. I carried him around on my hip forever."

"You miss your family." It wasn't a question. It was a statement.

For a brief moment she wanted to lie and say that she didn't, that the McCrays meant nothing to her anymore. But she was a McCray and she always would be, as she'd told Phoenix once before.

"I miss my mom and Maribel." Even saying the words created a hollow feeling in her stomach.

"Didn't your mom die a few years ago?"

She shifted uneasily and drew her knees up into a more comfortable position. "Yes. I was told not to come to the funeral. I wasn't welcome."

"That had to have hurt."

"Yeah." She stared down at her hands that she'd curled into fists, hardly believing she was telling Phoenix about her family. But then there was so much in her she needed to say, and he was listening. And easy to talk to. She'd probably lost perspective about twenty-four hours ago.

"What happened to your marriage?"

She closed her eyes tight, trying not to think about that time of her life. But it was like a sore inside her needing to bleed to heal. Before she knew it, words tumbled out. "When I was eighteen and graduated high school, the ranch was in financial trouble. My dad went to several banks and they wouldn't loan him any more money. He was so angry he accidentally slammed his hand in his truck door and broke two fingers. I drove him to another bank in Austin so he could talk to someone about a loan. That someone was Derek Wilcott. His family owned the bank."

"That's the man you married?"

"Yes." She opened her eyes and watched as Dixie tugged on Jake's jeans. Jake rolled over, laughing. Happy. It was a beautiful sound and warmed her heart. Every child should be happy.

"Rosie?" Phoenix murmured in a low voice as if to console her in some way. She turned her attention to him.

"Derek liked me, as my father put it. He and my father made a deal. He would give the family a large sum of money for my hand in marriage. That is, if I was still a virgin."

She looked into Phoenix's eyes as she said the words,

and she didn't see pity or sympathy. All she saw was concern, and it gave her the courage to continue. "I couldn't talk my dad out of it, so I begged my mother to intervene. She refused. She said the bank was going to foreclose on the ranch if I didn't. The whole family would have nowhere to go. I had to do it for the good of the family. I'd live in a mansion, have servants and my life would be good. She didn't see it as a hardship for me. She saw it as a fairy tale.

"It was a nightmare. My wedding night was horrific. Derek's idea of foreplay was to hurt me and to make me cry out in pain. He started beating me from the start and there was nothing I could do about it. He had me watched twenty-four hours a day, and I was in hell. Pure hell, and there was no way out. I…"

Phoenix scooted across the sofa and wrapped an arm around her, and she rested her face on his chest, feeling comfort like she'd never had before. "You don't have to say any more." He stroked her hair away from her face; his gentle touch was the healing power on the scars of her life.

She raised her head and wiped away an errant tear. "I have to say it all. I've kept it inside for so long, and I need to say the words out loud." She rested against him, loving the strength of his chest, the power of his arms and the soothing comfort of his presence.

"I got pregnant right away and I thought he would leave me alone then, but he didn't, and I feared for the safety of the baby. That's when I made the decision to leave. I started saving the money he gave me. I didn't know where I was going, but I was leaving before the baby was born. I was about eight months along when he came in one evening drunk. The gardener was still outside, and Derek accused me of having an affair with the man. He beat me senseless. I woke up in a pool of blood and managed to crawl to the phone and call 911. I was so worried about the baby, but I knew the truth before we reached the hospital. My baby was…my baby girl was dead." Another tear slipped from her eye, and Phoenix held her tight. She prayed she wouldn't start crying like she had so many other times.

"I'm sorry. That's why you were looking at all the baby girl stuff in Walmart."

"Yes." She sniffed into his chest. "I can never resist when I go into a store with baby things. I guess I'll always do that and wonder what my baby would have been like."

"What happened to your husband?"

"He was drunk upstairs and still had blood on him— my blood. He was arrested. His family tried to make me out as a slut to get him off, but I got a shark of an attorney and she went after the family big time. I was granted a divorce, and the family settled out of court with a lump sum of money."

"What happened to Derek?"

"He received an eight-year sentence but only served two years before the family's attorney got him out."

"And you used the money you received to start a new life?"

She pulled away from him, needing to get perspective once again. "No. I saved a little to start over, but the majority of the money I sent home to my dad. He had told me in the hospital that I had betrayed the family and I wasn't welcome at home."

"After what you'd been through? How could he say that?"

"The Wilcott family pulled the plug on the financial

support for the family after Derek was arrested, and the ranch was in jeopardy once again. My father said that I was selfish, thinking only of myself, and that I should have been a better wife, supporting my husband and learning to please him. I wanted to throw up."

"Then why send him the money?"

"My mother was there, and I didn't want her to lose her home because…because of me."

"Did you talk to your father after he received the money?"

"No. I've never heard a word from him, but he cashed the check."

"Oh, Rosie." His arm tightened around her, and the feel of it made her stronger. "I've never liked Ira McCray, and today I like him even less."

Outside the sun had snuck away and left darkness in its wake. Rosie shivered. Usually at this time of night she felt a little afraid.

"Hey, what's wrong?"

It felt strange to have someone to talk to, and she snuggled closer to Phoenix. "I'm not fond of the darkness. It hides all the bad and the unknown. When Derek was released from prison, I stayed awake at night and slept in the mornings. I bought a gun to protect myself in case he came looking for me."

"Did you have contact with him?"

"No. I heard he got married six months later, and his family moved him to Florida, where they have banks, too."

She sat up and straightened her hair, which had come undone and tumbled down her back. "I can't believe I've talked so much about myself."

He brushed her hair from her face, and she trembled

from the pleasure of it. The darkness wasn't daunting at all with Phoenix beside her. As the thought ran through her mind, she realized she was getting involved too fast. She was starved for emotional contact, and she had to back off to save her own sanity. She couldn't allow herself to be hurt again.

She got to her feet. "I think you'd better go. It's getting late, and didn't you say your family would be worried about you and Jake?"

"I'm more worried about you now."

She straightened her backbone. "Phoenix, I do not need someone to save me. I'm capable of doing that on my own."

"Whoa." He got to his feet and stood way too close. She wanted to take a step backward, but she wasn't that weak. "Where's that coming from? We were just talking like friends do."

"We're not friends, Phoenix."

"Rosie." He sighed. "Let's don't go back to being enemies. We've taken a giant leap forward. Let's stay there and explore the possibilities."

She grinned. His charm oozed from him like fluffs of whipped cream, and all she had to do was lick it up.

He leaned in, and he dipped his head to kiss her briefly. At the touch of his lips, a bolt of fear shot through her, but she didn't move away. *Phoenix isn't Derek.* He waited for her to step back, to resist, but she found she couldn't do either. The touch and taste of him on her lips were tempting, not frightening. And she wanted more. She looked up and he covered her mouth with his.

And just like that, she fell into his arms and was completely lost in the sensual feeling of her body against his. This was the way love was supposed to be between a man and woman: gentle, consensual and exciting. She wrapped her arms around his neck and held her body as close to him as she could. His muscles pressed into hers, as did his belt buckle, which oddly was an erotic sensation. The cowboy was taking her breath away and he'd just branded her with the biggest buckle in the world.

His lips trailed from hers to her cheek to her neck and lower to her breast. The world started to spin away as emotions too long denied swamped her. She couldn't think, could only feel. And the feeling was everything she ever dreamed it would be. Just when she thought his touch would take her away, a little voice interrupted.

"Dad-dy."

Jake wedged himself between them, wrapping his arms around Phoenix's legs. Reluctantly Phoenix pulled away and looked down at his son.

"Beer, Dad-dy."

It gave Rosie time to gain control, and she stepped away, straightening her blouse. She had to stop. He was a Rebel, so wrong for her. "I think you'd better take him home."

"Rosie."

She held up a hand. "No. You really need to go, and we really need to stop what we're doing. I mean it. We're getting involved too fast. Too deep. We need some time apart, and I need time to get my head straight."

"Ah, Rosie."

"Phoenix, please."

He picked up Jake. "This isn't over, Rosie, and we both know it." He walked over to the table and grabbed Jake's boots and the diaper bag. "I know you're scared, and I'll give you some space for now." He said to Jake, "Tell Rosie goodbye."

Jake leaned over to kiss her, and she kissed his cheek. "Goodbye, Jake." In doing so she was very close to Phoenix, and she got a whiff of his masculine scent. Her resolve weakened. Before she could pull away, Phoenix kissed the side of her face and rested his cheek against hers. His stubble brushed against her skin and she was lost.

"I know you have doubts about this relationship, but I will never hurt you."

"Phoenix."

He walked out the door and closed it. She stood there feeling lonelier than she had in a long time. Dixie barked and she reached down to pick her up, holding her just to steady her own nerves. The trailer became quiet. So quiet it made her jumpy. All the fun, all the energy, all the happiness of the day had gone, and she was left alone to deal with her lonely life.

A tear slipped from her eyes. She curled up in her chair, cuddling Dixie and wondering how she'd gotten so emotionally involved in such a short amount of time. So much so she'd told Phoenix everything about herself. Almost. She hadn't told him the deepest wound inside her.

And she never would.

# Chapter Nine

When Phoenix made it to the ranch, Jake was sound asleep in his car seat. It had been so hard for Phoenix to leave Rosie, but he knew she was right. They were getting involved too fast, and he had to think about Jake and what was best for him. But man, it hurt to leave her.

He sat in his truck for a while, resisting the urge to go back and talk to her. There was just something so sad about her in the dark in that trailer all alone. He'd never dreamed her life had been so horrific and her father had traded her like a prized horse. She deserved better than that. She deserved better than living in that trailer.

Kissing her was like the taste of springwater after a drought—fresh and soothing, and his thirst for her was insatiable. He just wanted to go on kissing her until there was no one but the two of them in the world. And that was probably the most romantic thing he'd ever thought in his whole life.

He'd often wondered how one fell in love, and he'd felt sure it would never happen to him. But Rosie's blue eyes hypnotized him. He liked her. He wanted to spend all his time with her just to see her smile. Just to see her happy. Most of his life he'd been only concerned about himself and the rodeo. It was a big eye-opener to have all these feelings for a woman he barely knew. Maybe it was the father thing bringing out the best in him. Or maybe it was just Rosie.

Pax was half-asleep on the sofa and Rico was reclining in his chair, watching TV. A big box sat in the middle of the den—Jake's things from Colorado had arrived. Jake was sound asleep on his shoulder, and he put him to bed.

After laying him in the crib, Phoenix stared at his son for a moment. He never knew he could love someone this much, but that little boy had opened up Phoenix's heart to a whole new world of feelings. He leaned over and kissed Jake's cheek.

"Love you, son. Good night." He covered him up and left the room.

In the den, Pax sat up and stretched. "That box came for you."

"It's Jake's stuff. I'll go through it later."

"Where are you going to put all of it? We're limited on room, Phoenix."

"I'll put it in my room, Pax. Don't worry about it."

Rico got up and headed for his room. "See you guys in the morning." Rico wasn't hanging around for a brothers' quarrel. At the door, he turned. "If you need to, you can store stuff in my room. I only need a place to sleep."

"Thank you, Rico." Phoenix looked at Paxton. "That's what family is all about."

"C'mon, Phoenix."

Phoenix didn't stay to listen to Pax. He was tired and would probably say things he'd regret, so he took a quick shower and went to bed. Thoughts of Rosie in the trailer plagued him. She needed a home with a big bathroom so she could bathe anytime she wanted.

As he drifted off to sleep, Rosie was there with her

long red hair flowing down her back, and she was smiling at him. That was all the comfort he needed to shut out the night.

THE NEXT MORNING when Phoenix woke, Jake was still asleep in his crib. He was tired from all the playing yesterday. Phoenix pulled on his jeans and went to fix breakfast. Paxton was sitting at the table, drinking coffee.

Phoenix grabbed orange juice from the refrigerator and then filled a cup with coffee. Leaning against the cabinet, he stared at the brother he spent most of his time with.

"Okay." Paxton threw up his hands. "I was a jerk last night. You can put some stuff in my room, too."

Phoenix took a sip of his coffee. "What is it with you? Why are you so testy about Jake?"

Pax leaned back in his chair, his brownish-blond hair falling in his eyes. "We've stayed focused and worked hard this year. Now your focus is somewhere else, and I'm worried about Vegas."

"I've had a slight detour, that's all. My focus is still on the rodeo, but my heart is with my son, and I'm doing everything I can to make sure he has a good life."

"We have a rodeo in Stephenville tomorrow. What are you going to do with Jake?"

"Take him with me."

Paxton frowned. "Are you serious? What are you going to do with him at a rodeo?"

"It's something I'll have to work out."

Pax leaned forward, a gleam in his eyes. "Here's a thought. Mom is dying to keep him, so why not let her? That way your focus will be completely on the rodeo."

"I can't leave Jake this soon."

"I've heard kids are very flexible. He may cry for a little bit, but then he'll settle down and get attached to Mom."

"Jake stays with me. I'm not passing him off like a football. I'm not shirking my responsibility."

Paxton stood, and Phoenix realized his brother was still in his underwear. "Then I'm going to kick your ass in Vegas."

"Oh yeah. Just try. And try wearing clothes when you come into the kitchen. I have a son in the house."

Pax shook his head. "I don't even know you anymore."

"Not again," Rico muttered, coming into the kitchen.

A loud cry took words right out of Phoenix's mouth, and he ran to the bedroom. Jake was standing in his crib, crying his little heart out.

"Hey, buddy. Everything's okay. Daddy's here."

"Dad-dy." Jake held out his arms, tears rolling down his cheeks.

Phoenix lifted him out of the baby bed and laid him on the big bed. He changed his diaper quickly without even holding his breath, carried him into the kitchen and put him in his high chair.

"Beer, Dad-dy."

Phoenix placed the sippy cup on the tray of the chair, and Jake grabbed it.

"I can't wait till Mom hears that," Paxton said from the doorway, fully dressed.

"Are you trying to get on my bad side this morning?"

Paxton didn't answer. He walked over to Jake. "Hey, Jake."

Jake held up the sippy cup. "Beer."

Paxton shook his head. "He's a cute little thing, isn't he?"

"He grows on you," Phoenix replied.

"Yeah. You're really good with him."

"And that surprises you?"

"Yeah. And I'm not saying that to be mean. I'm trying to come to grips with this, too."

"Breakfast," Rico said from the stove. "Round three can wait till later."

After breakfast, Jericho and Paxton got ready to leave for the day.

"I've set up an appointment for Jake to see a pediatrician, but I'll try to catch y'all later."

Paxton placed his hat on his head. "Good."

The morning was spent at the doctor's office, where Phoenix and Jake got acquainted with the pediatrician who would be taking care of Jake. Phoenix had Jake's medical file from Mrs. Green and everything went smoothly. Jake was a healthy little boy. Phoenix was glad to hear that.

When they got back to the house, Phoenix unpacked the box. Jake was excited and danced around the box as he recognized his things, pulling out toys and stuffed animals. Phoenix knelt on the floor and watched the happiness on his son's face. It was clear in his bright brown eyes that his possessions made a world of difference. Something familiar. Something Jake could identify with. He pulled out some DVDs and giggled. He ran to the DVD player and tried to push one in, case and all.

"Hey, Daddy will do that." Phoenix opened the case, inserted the disc and turned on the TV. SpongeBob SquarePants popped onto the screen. Jake sat in front of the TV, mesmerized. Everything else was forgotten. Phoenix managed to get most of the stuff put up in his room. The toys he left in the den because he knew Jake would want to play with them.

After Jake's nap, Phoenix dressed him in his boots and jeans, and they headed for the barn to saddle up and join the family working on the ranch. Jake sat in front of him, his eyes as big as saucers as he gripped the saddle horn.

"Horse."

As they rode, Phoenix enjoyed being back in the saddle. He was a cowboy to his soul. A gentle breeze rustled the leaves that still clung to the tall oaks. Soon they would fall to the ground in a bed of oranges and browns. The fresh air was like nothing on earth, clean and invigorating, and it filled his lungs. He took a well-used trail, crossed a creek and rode on.

"Wa-wa."

"Yes, that's a creek. Yaupon Creek."

A jackrabbit jumped out in front of them.

"Bunny," Jake said.

Dust billowed in the distance, signaling they'd reached the roundup site. The bellowing of calves and cows followed, as did the stench of manure.

"Cow."

As they rode closer, he could see his mom and Grandpa standing under an oak. A blanket lay on the ground with a picnic basket. His mother usually brought lunch during roundup when they were far away from the house.

"Oh, I'm so glad you brought him." His mother held out her arms and Jake went to her.

"I'm going to help for a while."

"You go ahead." Grandpa waved him away. "We'll take care of this little whippersnapper."

Phoenix dismounted, crawled into the portable pens with his brothers and helped tag, vaccinate and castrate calves. He could taste dust in his mouth and the bellowing of cows was deafening in his ears, but he continued his work. Above the bellows, he heard a wail and glanced up to see Jake running for the pen with his mother behind him. Horses were lined up along the fence, and Jake was headed right for them.

"Oh, man." He jumped over the fence and started to run, his chaps flapping around his legs as he intercepted Jake before he reached the horses. He swung the boy up into his arms. Tears ran down Jake's cheeks and loud wails erupted from his chest.

"Dad-dy. Dad-dy. Dad-dy."

Phoenix patted Jake's back. "It's okay. Daddy's here." He'd been right. It was too soon for Jake to be separated from him.

"I'm taking him back to the house!" he shouted to his brothers.

"Go ahead!" Falcon shouted back.

"I got you covered," Elias said.

"I'll do his part," Paxton piped up.

"And who'll do yours?"

"Shut up, Elias."

And all was well with the Rebel brothers.

"I'm so sorry, son." His mother finally reached them. "He just got away from us."

"He's known for that, Mom. Don't worry about it."

"You take care of your son and don't worry about the ranch. There's plenty of us to do that."

"Thanks, Mom."

He mounted up. Jake refused to sit facing the saddle horn. He buried his face in Phoenix's chest and clung to him like a leech. He stayed in that position all the way to the ranch, and Phoenix had to make him sit on a bale of hay so he could unsaddle the horse.

Back at the bunkhouse, Jake still clung to him. Phoenix didn't understand what had upset him so much. Maybe it was the strange environment and the fact that he couldn't see his father. Phoenix held him a little tighter, wanting to reassure him. Jake's heart beat against Phoenix's in perfect time. As he felt that little thudding, he realized just how much he loved this little boy. He would do anything for him. His son had suddenly become his whole life.

After that thought, his mind turned to last night and Rosie's heart beating against his in perfect harmony. His belt buckle had pressed into her flesh almost like a brand, and he felt a connection like he'd never felt before. *He loved her.*

It took a moment for the truth of that to sink in. From the moment she'd rounded his truck with her blue eyes blazing like a Colt .45, they'd made a connection. It didn't matter what her name was. It mattered only that they loved each other.

He wasn't sure how she felt, but he was making inroads into her resolve to stay away from a Rebel. He would give her time. But not too long.

"Beer, Dad-dy."

Phoenix lifted Jake's chin so he could look into his eyes. "Milk."

"Beer."

Phoenix had a feeling he wasn't going to win this battle. He went into the kitchen to fill the sippy cup.

With SpongeBob SquarePants on the TV and Jake in front of it, the stress of the afternoon faded away. Soon Jake was running around the room, playing with his toys, and Phoenix breathed a sigh of relief. He pulled his phone out of his back pocket and laid it on the counter. He wanted to call Rosie and tell her about his afternoon. But he'd promised and he wasn't going back on his word. He wondered if she missed him as much as he missed her. His life had taken a one-hundred-eighty-degree turn in the past few days and he wasn't complaining. He rather liked the change.

THE NEXT MORNING they left for a rodeo in Stephenville, Texas. Phoenix had to pack a lot of stuff for Jake, so they were late getting away. The backseat of the truck was packed with kid stuff and diapers. He wanted to make sure he had enough diapers to last the weekend. They said goodbye to the family, and off they went to another rodeo. This time it was a little different. They had an extra passenger.

The drive was uneventful. Once they reached Stephenville, Paxton went to check them in and get their numbers while Phoenix took care of Jake.

He met Cole Bryant and Dakota Janaway, two bull riders, and talked for a few minutes about rodeo. He introduced Jake, and Jake shied away and buried his head in Phoenix's shoulder. Bored with the talk, Jake wanted down.

"Stay right here," he told him.

"This is a new Phoenix," Cole joked. "I don't think I know him."

"Let me tell you, it's a job taking care of a child."

"Cowboys usually have wives to take on the role," Dakota said.

"Yeah." Phoenix looked down and Jake wasn't there. "Where did he go that fast? Jake? Help me look. He has to be here somewhere." The cowboys spread out and started to look for the boy.

"Jake!" Phoenix ran through cowboys and cowgirls

milling around, looking and looking, but Jake was nowhere to be found. His heart pounded like a steam engine and he felt sure smoke was coming out of his ears in frustration. Where was his kid? He turned and let out a long breath. A beautiful redhead strolled toward him with Jake in her arms.

*Rosie.*

"Are you missing someone?" Her blue eyes were bright and sparkled with merriment. Had it been only a day since he'd seen her? He was starved for her presence.

"Yes, a lot." His eyes never wavered from hers, and they both knew he wasn't talking about Jake.

"Dad-dy."

Phoenix turned his attention to his son. "I'm upset with you. You're not supposed to run from Daddy."

Jake's bottom lip trembled at the sternness of Phoenix's words.

"Phoenix," Rosie said softly, and the fear in him subsided. "He must've seen me in the crowd and came running. He didn't know he was doing anything wrong."

Jake held out his arms and Phoenix took him. "You scared Daddy."

"Ro-sie." Jake pointed.

Phoenix knew there was no use trying to discipline Jake. He was too young to understand, but he would have to start discipline sometime soon. Just not today.

"You're looking good." His eyes traveled over her tight Wranglers that clung to every curve. A turquoise ribbon held back her long hair, and she was probably wearing that color when she rode tonight. It made her blue eyes stand out.

"Phoenix." A throaty whisper echoed in her voice.

"What?"

"You're so obvious. I don't know why I'm attracted to you."

"I know why. You're hot and I'm horny."

She laughed, a bubbly sound that seemed to surprise her. "We'll discuss that later."

Reaching out, she caressed Jake's cheek. There was so much meaning in the word *later*, it took a moment for him to recover.

"What are you going to do with Jake when you ride?"

"Paxton and I are going to trade off taking care of him."

"Don't you usually help each other in the chute with the bull rope and such?"

"Yeah, but I was hoping Jake would stay with one of the cowboys."

She shook her head. "Cowboy, you haven't thought this through, have you?"

"My game plan is to improvise as I go along because I'm not leaving Jake back at the ranch."

She patted Jake's back. "I'll take care of him."

He stared at her. "So...so what about the Rebel/Mc-Cray thing? No more doubts about us?"

"Oh, still lots of doubts, but I'm a sucker for this little guy." She kissed Jake and smiled at Phoenix. "His dad's not too bad, either. Later, cowboy."

She walked off, and Phoenix watched the sway of her hips. His day had just gotten a whole lot better.

## Chapter Ten

Rosie had every intention of staying away from Phoenix. But once he and Jake left on Wednesday, she'd felt as if the sunshine had gone out of her world. It was lonely, and she kept listening for the sound of Phoenix's truck the next day. She didn't understand why she was depriving herself of something that made her feel so good. The Rebel/McCray feud had nothing to do with her. Her father had disowned her and she had a right to make her own choices.

The moment she saw Jake running toward her, she knew she wanted that little boy and his father in her life. She was willing to take a risk to make it happen. Then she saw Phoenix's worried expression. He needed her help, and no one had ever needed her like that before.

Rosie hurried to her trailer and dressed for the night. Then she made her way to the rodeo and rushed to get ready for her race. Lady knew what to do. All Rosie had to do was guide her. She blasted out and made the run in fourteen point six seconds. She would have to do better to win in Vegas. Everyone's attention was now on the National Finals Rodeo.

After taking care of Lady, Rosie hurried back to get

Jake so Phoenix could bull-ride. Jake was half asleep on Phoenix's shoulder.

"He's tired and sleepy, but he hasn't eaten yet."

Rosie took the baby into her arms. "I'll take him to my trailer and get him ready for bed. Where are his pajamas?"

Phoenix held up the diaper bag. "Everything's in here."

She hated she had to miss Phoenix's ride, but there would be other times. Right now Jake needed to go to bed.

An hour later, Phoenix tapped on her door and came in. He brought the cool outdoors and a whole lot of sunshine, even though it was dark, into the small trailer.

She'd changed into shorts and a tank top because she'd given Jake a bath. The sofa made into a half bed and that's where Jake was curled up with Floppy, his SpongeBob blanket and Dixie. The moment Jake saw Phoenix he sat up and called, "Dad-dy." He'd been asking for Phoenix ever since she'd dressed him in his pajamas. Once again she admired Phoenix and his gentleness with his son.

He sat on the bed and gathered Jake into his arms. "Hey, buddy!"

Jake rested his head on Phoenix's shoulder. "Dad-dy." In minutes Jake was sound asleep.

Phoenix gently laid him on the sofa bed and covered him with a blanket. "Thanks." He looked at her, and the fire in his eyes lit a fuse in her that had been dormant for a long time. "I could not have done this without you. I don't know what I was thinking."

She sat in her chair, which was inches from him, and curled her feet beneath her. "I'm not going to criticize because I admire what you're doing. Most cowboys I know would have left Jake with their mothers."

Phoenix glanced at his son. "I've got one more rodeo before the finals, and then I'll have to think about quitting. Jake comes first, and he needs to be in bed by nine o'clock."

"You can do it and I'll help. It wasn't too bad tonight. Jake just got tired."

He grimaced. "Do you mind if I pull off my boots? I've had a shower, and now I just want to relax."

"Sure." There was something intimate about a cowboy removing his boots in her trailer. That signified an intimacy they hadn't reached yet. But they were getting close, and Rosie wasn't afraid. She just knew she could trust this cowboy with her heart.

He scooted back and rested his head against the sofa, his eyes on her. "You look different tonight."

"I had to change clothes to give Jake a bath."

"How did you do that in a shower?"

"I have a handheld nozzle to save water. I just soaped him up and rinsed it off. He thought it was fun. He giggled a lot when I sprayed water over his head. Dixie barked the whole time."

"They make a team, don't they?" Phoenix glanced toward Dixie, who was curled up against Jake.

"Do you remember much about Jake's mother?" She didn't mean to change the subject so abruptly, but she was curious.

"Not much, I'm ashamed to say. It was just sex, and that bothers me sometimes. The responsible part kicks in every now and then."

"My daughter was conceived the same way and I loved her with all my heart, so I don't think it matters."

He leaned forward and brushed hair away from her face. "I'm sorry about your daughter."

"I bought so many baby things and…" Tears clogged her throat and she couldn't go on.

Phoenix slipped into the chair with her. She scooted onto his lap and leaned against him like a child needing comfort. And she should have been past that.

"Would you do something for me?"

"What?" she whispered into his chest.

"Stop being sad and rejoice in the fact that you had a child to remember. A child you loved. It's time to move on, Rosie. It's time."

She lifted her head and stared into his dark eyes. "I was thinking the same thing. My baby is in a secret place in my heart and she will always be there, but the rest of my heart is still alive and needs…"

He placed his hand above her breast, and she felt her heart beating against his palm like thunder, loud and frightening. "Needs what?"

"Needs to feel again."

With his other hand he threaded his fingers through her hair and tucked it behind her ear. His lips gently touched hers, so gently that it annoyed her. She didn't want him to be patient and understanding. She wanted him to treat her like the girls he'd dated. The girls he wanted to make love to. That's what she wanted: to feel all those emotions she'd heard about. To feel them with Phoenix.

"You're so beautiful, and I love your hair."

"I've hated my hair all my life."

"Why? It's gorgeous. Long and straight and a coppery color I've never seen before."

"Phoenix…"

She knew what he was doing, giving her time to

think or maybe change her mind. But she knew what she wanted.

She wrapped her arms around his neck and kissed him boldly and without shame. He kissed her back with equal fervor. He tasted of peppermint and orange juice…

"Orange juice," she whispered between kisses.

"Mmm. I drink a lot of OJ."

His lips covered hers and all other thought left her. Wonderful dizzying feelings flowed through her. New and unchartered emotions made the blood sing in her veins and her heart dance in a crazy rhythm that was driving her wild.

He rested his face in the warmth of her neck, and she knew she needed to tell him some things before they went any further.

"You taste like chocolate," he murmured throatily.

"Jake wanted a chocolate chip cookie and I ate most of it."

"Mmm."

"Phoenix…"

"Hmm?"

As he nibbled on her earlobe, she forgot what she wanted to talk about. But then it came roaring back. "I… I don't enjoy…sex."

He lifted his head. His dark hair was tousled across his forehead and his eyes were full of passion. "What?"

"Sex was awful with Derek and I was always glad when it was over. I never enjoyed it like a woman is supposed to, and I worry that I may never…"

"Shh." He placed a finger over her lips. "We'll take it slow and easy and if you want to stop, we'll stop. You just need to relax and stop worrying and let it happen."

She nestled her face against his. "There's this little

seed of doubt in me that says I shouldn't be doing anything with you but showing you the door. I ignore it most of the time."

"I feel the Rebel/McCray thing, too. I don't give it much attention, either. Yesterday I was holding Jake and felt his heart beat against mine and realized how much I loved that kid. At the same time I thought about the night before when I held you and felt your heart beat in perfect rhythm with mine. A powerful thing is happening between us. I've never been in love, Rosie, but what I feel for you I think is love. The real thing. Like one hundred percent."

"Oh, Phoenix."

"So let's just take it slow and live in the moment and be grateful we found each other."

"Life is not that simple."

"No, but love is."

She threw back her head and laughed, a bubbly sound that rushed through her whole body like sweet, sweet wine, reviving her dormant senses.

Phoenix rained kisses all the way to her chin. "What's so funny?"

"You and your positive attitude. You make me laugh and you make me happy. I just want to keep on laughing because I've been silent for too long."

He tickled her rib cage, and she squirmed and giggled like a teenager who was over the moon in love. His hand slipped to her breast and cupped it.

"Phoenix." Her breath caught in her throat at the exquisite sensation. "We're going to wake Jake."

"Nah. Once he goes to sleep he's out for the night." He stood and threw her over his shoulder, patting her butt. "This is our time." He stopped to lock the door and put on the safety chain, then strolled with her to the small bedroom. She had no objections.

A part of her was eager and the other was hesitant, but she knew she wanted to experience sex with a man she cared about. She was twenty-eight years old and it was long overdue. She didn't know what to expect, and she tensed as his naked body touched hers. But only for a moment. The minute she touched his whipcord muscles, her body ached for something more than what she'd known.

His touch was gentle at first as if he was memorizing every curve, every intimate part of her. And she enjoyed it. She enjoyed being touched, being with a man of her choosing. In turn she touched him boldly and wanted to keep on touching, stroking his hard muscles. This was the way it was supposed to be between a man and a woman. Needing. Loving.

When he kissed her deeply, she kissed him back with all the fervor that was in her heart. It was drugging, yet uplifting, and she ran her hands through his hair and then down his chest just to feel his heart beating strongly against her.

He rolled onto her and she welcomed him. She didn't shy away or beg him to stop. And what happened next was unlike anything she'd ever experienced. Her muscles didn't tense. The two of them made love just like it was supposed to be made. Just like she'd heard about. And when the pleasure came, fireworks seemed to dance in her mind and explode along her nerve endings. It was the best feeling she'd ever felt in her life. She clung to Phoenix because she needed to hold on to something strong and powerful. And all man.

He held her for a long time afterward, gently kissing her and stroking her skin. "Are you okay?"

"I'm on top of the world, so you'd better pull me down before I float away."

He laughed into her throat. "That good, huh?"

"Like fireworks on the Fourth of July."

He snuggled further into the bed and wrapped his arms around her. "Let's make every day the Fourth of July."

She sighed and kissed his lips slowly. "I love you."

He pushed her long hair away from her face and kissed the side of her face. "I love you, too."

Rosie drifted off to sleep with those words playing like a song in her head that would keep her happy for the rest of her life.

PHOENIX LAY AWAKE a long time after Rosie went to sleep. For the first time in his life, he didn't think about himself or his pleasure. He thought about Rosie and wanted it to be special for her. Her ex had done a number on her, and she deserved to know sex the way it should be. Not with violence and hatred. And it was just as she'd said. Like fireworks. He'd known it would be that way the moment he'd looked into her blue eyes. Their connection was strong and he wanted it to stay that way.

He'd been with a lot of other girls and that bothered him, but he couldn't go back and change it. He knew, though, Rosie would be his last. He would be faithful to her just like his dad had been to his mother. When a Rebel loved, he loved forever. His dad had said that to him and his brothers so many times that it was like a brand on his brain. Now Phoenix knew what it meant.

He slowly gave in to the tiredness pulling at him.

A long time later, Rosie woke him and rained kisses along his jaw. He turned to her.

"Are you asleep?" she asked shyly.

"Not anymore. You know, I'm the match and you're the flame. You can light me up anytime you want."

She laughed and they started the party all over again.

The next time he awoke, he crawled out of bed and reached for his underwear.

"Where are you going?" Rosie asked.

"To get the little guy. If he wakes up and I'm not there, he might be upset. He usually crawls into bed with me about five."

She sat up. "That's what I love most about you—your devotion to your son."

Phoenix gathered Jake into his arms, carried him back to the bed and laid him between them. The boy never woke up. Dixie jumped up beside Rosie, and Phoenix pulled the sheet over them. He snuggled down to get a couple more hours of sleep.

Jake curled into him, and Phoenix reached out and stroked Rosie's cheek. She kissed his hand. He thought if life could stay this way, he would be happy. But he knew that was wishful thinking. Sometime soon he would have to broach the subject of Rosie with his mother. The younger, immature Phoenix would shy away from that. But the new and improved Phoenix had to face her and explain that he'd fallen in love with the niece of the man who'd tried to kill him as a boy. He'd fallen in love with a McCray.

## Chapter Eleven

Rosie was happier than she'd ever been in her life. She'd forgotten what it was like to feel joy and love for someone else. After their father had kicked her sister, Maribel, out of the house, all the joy in Rosie's life had disappeared. She'd cried herself to sleep for a solid month, but Maribel never came home. Her mother cried, too. Her dad never changed his mind, though.

Maribel had gotten pregnant in high school, and their father had called her trash and told her to leave unless she told him the name of the father. Maribel had refused. The day her sister had left with a small suitcase was the day the sun started to dim in Rosie's life. A few years later her father had married Rosie off to Derek, and the sun had completely disappeared.

But now...

A smile threatened her lips, and she had an urge to break out into song. She was happy. And it was the best feeling in the world.

She and Phoenix spent every moment of the weekend together, rodeoing and rushing back to the trailer to be alone. Haley stopped by on Saturday afternoon when Phoenix was lazing on the sofa bed with Jake. She was startled to see Phoenix there but Rosie didn't feel any embarrassment. She didn't mind that people knew they were together. Haley left quickly, and Rosie fell onto the sofa beside Phoenix, laughing.

"Everyone will know now," Phoenix said. "Do you mind?"

"No." She straightened up and Jake crawled onto her lap.

"Horse." He showed her the toy animal in his hand.

"Yes." She kissed his cheek and resisted the urge to giggle. Happiness was turning her into a silly teenager. She welcomed the feeling of being uninhibited and free and doing exactly what she wanted. And what she wanted was Phoenix.

Sunday morning was bittersweet as they packed up to head home. They shared a long kiss inside the trailer, saying goodbye. They kissed so long that Jake wedged himself between them, wanting attention.

Phoenix swung the boy up into his arms. "We have lunch with Mom, and I'll call you afterward." One more quick kiss and he was gone.

The trailer was lonely and quiet again, and the sun had temporarily vanished. How had she lived by herself for so long? She wanted to run out the door and beg Phoenix to come back. But she resisted. She would see him again and soon. She held on to that as she secured cabinets and put everything away for the trip home.

THEY MADE IT home in time for lunch with the family, and Phoenix was antsy. He wanted to get it over with so he could go see Rosie. He'd been away from her only for about three hours, but that seemed too long.

Jake sat beside him in a high chair, picking up pieces of roast with his fingers. John sat in another high chair on the other end of the table, doing the same thing. John soon grew tired and wanted down. He held his arms out to Leah.

"Momma. Momma. Momma."

"No," Falcon said. "Stay in your chair. Eat your lunch."

John stuck out his lip and wailed, "Momma! Momma! Momma!"

"Falcon?" Leah appealed to her husband.

"No, Leah. He stays in his chair. He has to learn discipline."

"Daddy?" Eden joined John's bandwagon.

Falcon pointed his fork at his daughter. "You stay in your chair, too."

Phoenix noticed Jake watching all of this, his eyes on John. Suddenly he pointed a finger at his cousin and said, "No!"

Everyone laughed and Jake laughed, too, although he had no idea what everyone was laughing about. Suddenly he turned to Phoenix. and said, "Beer, Dad-dy."

The room became so quiet, Phoenix could hear himself breathing. Words rushed to his throat, but before he could voice any of them, his mother spoke up.

"Phoenix, are you giving this baby beer?"

"Of course not." He got up and went into the kitchen to get Jake's sippy cup and milk.

When he came back, Paxton was telling the story about the beer and getting Jake off a bottle. "It worked, too."

"Only Phoenix would think of something like that," Falcon remarked.

"Son, if you'd just asked me, I could have helped you."

"I figured it out on my own, Mom, and that's what I wanted to do."

He placed the sippy cup in front of Jake. His son took a big swig and then pointed at Leah and said, "Ro-sie."

Phoenix tensed. He should tell his mom about Rosie, but he didn't want to do that in front of everyone. He would do it later when they were alone. Her reaction wasn't going to be good, and he had to be prepared to stand up to his mother.

"No," he said to Jake. "That's Aunt Leah."

"Mom-ma."

"No," Phoenix said again. "That's Aunt Leah."

"Who's Rosie?" his mother asked.

"She's a barrel racer who helped me with Jake at the rodeo this weekend." That was all he was willing to say at this point.

"Do you know Rosie, Paxton?" His mother focused on Paxton since she knew she wasn't going to get anything out of Phoenix.

"Uh...uh...yeah. I know her. She's nice and good with Jake."

"Do you know her, Eden?" His mother wanted information and she was going to get it any way she could, but he knew he could depend on Paxton and Eden to be discreet.

"Yes, Grandma. She's a barrel racer and really good."

"Mom, what's the big deal?" Falcon asked.

"I'm just afraid Phoenix is getting involved with someone too quickly."

Phoenix had had enough. He took Jake out of his chair. "Since I'm the baby of the family, I know it's hard for you to realize that I'm a grown man and I can make my own decisions. Rosie was nice enough to help me and I appreciated it. I couldn't ride unless someone took care of him, and she offered. That's all I'm going to say. Now I'm leaving. It's time for Jake's nap."

"Phoenix," his mom called after him, but he didn't stop. He had to make a stand and soon, but he felt he had to do that alone so he could explain exactly how he felt.

Paxton followed him to the bunkhouse. "Man, that was close. Mom's watching you like a hawk."

"Sorry you got caught in the middle."

"No problem."

Phoenix changed Jake's diaper and was about to put him in his crib when he thought he really needed to see Rosie. Jake could nap there. He started throwing things into the diaper bag.

"Where are you going?"

He glanced at his brother lounging on the sofa. "It's best if you don't know."

"Ah, Phoenix, can't you see this is wrong and it's only going to hurt you and Rosie? I'm an expert at the hurt thing, and you've got a whole lot of hurt waiting on you. Mom will never accept Rosie. You have to understand that."

He picked up the diaper bag and Jake. "If anyone asks, you don't know where I am."

"That's my motto. I don't know a thing."

He tried not to think on the way to Rosie's, but Paxton was right. He had to find a way to break the news to his mother without all of them getting hurt. He wasn't sure there was a way, but he knew no matter what it took, he was going to be with Rosie. He loved her. He wondered how many men had said those words and then eventually had their insides cave in from the pain. He was willing to take the risk.

Rosie had parked her trailer by the barn and then gone into town to buy groceries. She was unloading the truck when Phoenix drove up. Her heart did a happy dance across her ribs, and she ran to meet him. He caught her and kissed her deeply and she held on for a moment longer.

"I've missed you," she whispered against his lips.

"Me, too." He rested his forehead against hers, and she breathed in the musky, masculine scent of him.

"Dad-dy. Dad-dy," Jake called.

"I have to get him out. I think he missed you as much as I did."

After undoing the car seat, he lifted Jake out onto the ground. He ran to Rosie and wrapped his arms around her knees. "Mom-ma. Mom-ma."

Rosie's heart stopped, and she glanced at Phoenix. "Did you tell him to call me that?"

Phoenix shook his head. "He heard John calling Leah that at lunch. I guess he's decided who's his mother."

A seed of doubt pierced her, and she hated that. "But, Phoenix…"

"What? You don't want to be his mother? I thought we were…"

"We are, but I'm so afraid. I never thought… It just… I don't know how to handle this."

"Mom-ma." Jake held up his arms.

She looked down into that baby face, and all her motherly instincts gathered force. There was no way she could reject this little boy. She loved him. She loved his father. She picked up Jake, accepting this wonderful gift. She just hated that she had doubts whether there was a future for them. But she would keep fighting for what she wanted.

The days that followed were a happy time—all the way. They spent every possible moment together, and it was more than Rosie had ever imagined a relationship between a man and a woman could be. She told Phoenix things about herself she'd never told anyone.

After lunch, when Jake took his nap, was their special time for talking, sharing and loving. They lay in bed and Rosie curled into Phoenix's side with her head on his chest.

"I need to tell you something."

He played with her hair. "What?"

"I had so many internal injuries from the beating, the doctor said it would be difficult for me to get pregnant again. Not impossible, but difficult. So I may never have another child. That hurts, and…"

He cupped her face in his hand. "It doesn't matter to me. I have one child I can barely take care of. If we never have another child, that would be fine with me. I love you, Rosie, and nothing else matters."

She believed him.

Snuggling closer, she said, "Tell me about the day you and your brother were shot by Ezra McCray."

"I don't remember much. Dad let us ride his horse while he worked near the McCray property. We jumped a couple of logs and I told Jude to try to jump the fence, but Jude said we'd get in trouble. I kept on badgering him, and finally we sailed over the fence onto McCray land. The horse was so fast Jude couldn't turn him, and then I heard a loud boom. I woke up in a hospital with my mom sobbing by my bed. My dad was so white, and I knew something bad had happened."

He took a deep breath. "If I hadn't urged Jude to jump the fence, none of the bad things would have happened.

The Rebels and McCrays would just be neighbors tolerating each other. Everything is my fault. Dad said it wasn't, but it was."

"Oh, Phoenix, you were a little boy. Uncle Ezra shot at children. That's all on him. Not you. My mom always said he was a little crazy after he lost the love of his life."

"Didn't he have a wife and kids?"

"Yeah, but he never got over his first love. Not sure what happened to her, if she died or what. I never asked."

His arm tightened around her. "I've been waiting for an opportunity to tell my mom about us, but there's always someone around. She's not going to take it well, and I want to do it privately. She blames the McCrays for everything bad in our lives, especially my dad's death. It's going to be hard on her."

She lifted her head and stared into his dark, warm eyes. "We can wait until you feel she's ready."

"But I don't want to wait on our lives. I want us to be together as a family. I'll tell her soon."

She listened with an aching heart, experiencing his pain, but she had to wonder if the Rebel/McCray feud would ever end. Or if it would completely destroy their love.

THEY WENT TO a rodeo the next weekend and used the same system as before. As soon as she finished barrel racing, she took Jake and put him down for the night. Everything was working well, and Rosie was beginning to think that maybe, just maybe, they might have a future.

October gave way to November and cooler temperatures. Phoenix was set to tell his mother about them, but she came down with the flu, and he thought he should wait until she felt better. Rosie hated that he was in such turmoil.

They lived in their own private cocoon of happiness, and she didn't want anything or anyone to intrude. She felt a part of a family for the first time in a long time. It felt good and right.

Jake was almost out of diapers, so they made the trip into Temple to stock up. They stopped for lunch, and once they were back in the truck, Phoenix just sat there.

She glanced at him. "Something wrong?"

He ran his hand over the steering wheel and then looked at her. "Don't freak out or anything when I say this, but I want to make a commitment to you. A real commitment that shows I'm serious about this relationship."

She touched his cheek and loved the feel of his roughened skin. "I know you're serious. I am, too."

"Then let's get a marriage license."

"Phoenix…"

"Hear me out. We can go to the county clerk in Belton, which is less than fifteen minutes away, and apply for one. I looked it up online, and all you need is a form of ID and your Social Security number. We don't have to get married right now, but we'll have the license, and we can do it whenever you want. I'll keep it in the glove compartment, and all you have to say is 'Let's do it.' I won't pressure you or anything. It'll just be a commitment between the two of us."

She was touched that he felt so deeply about it. Then the doubts began to take hold, and she wasn't sure what she wanted to do. "Phoenix, that's crazy."

He cupped her face with one hand. "Be crazy with me."

The look in his eyes obliterated any doubt she had.

"We have to wait seventy-two hours for the license to be official," he said, "and it lasts for thirty days. That gives us time to think and decide about our future."

"I'm as crazy as you, because I'm thinking about it."

Twenty minutes later, they were in the clerk's office with Jake, filling out the application. She felt giddy and silly and happy all at the same time. Once they were back in the truck, Phoenix put the license in the glove compartment.

"It's up to you. When you're ready, all you have to do is say the word, because you know I love you."

They stared at each other and she smiled. "I'm with you all the way, cowboy."

After that, they didn't talk about the license. They just enjoyed their time together. But Rosie thought of it often, and she was close to saying yes.

THEY'D SPENT THE afternoon at a local carnival, and Jake had the time of his life riding the carousel, the flying elephants, the train and the cars. He wasn't afraid of anything, and she was sure he got it from his daredevil father.

They ate yucky stuff like cotton candy, and she was never going to get the pink off Jake's face. It was a fun afternoon. They laughed at Jake and each other and just enjoyed being a family.

*A family.* That's what she wanted more than anything in the world. Her own family. And she had that with Phoenix and Jake. But there was that doubt again, just beyond her subconscious, wanting to snatch her joy away.

Jake had fallen asleep on the way home and Rosie had put him down for a nap. It was late, but he was worn out. Dixie was standing guard. Rosie hurried to join Phoenix. A noise grabbed her attention and she glanced back.

Her father and her brother, Gunnar, stood at the edge of the trailer.

She shivered. What were they doing here? How had they found her?

At the corral, Phoenix was wrapping the water pipes for the winter. He stood frozen as he noticed the men. But he quickly came toward her.

Her father stepped forward with a frown she knew well. She couldn't ever remember her father smiling. He nodded toward Phoenix. "I'm only going to tell you this once, girl. Stay away from him or he'll never make it to Vegas."

Phoenix made it to her side before she could respond... "I think you'd better stop making threats and leave. You're not scaring anyone."

Gunnar got in Phoenix's face. "If you like breathing, you'd better do what he says."

"What is it to you, Gunnar? Your father has disowned Rosie, so what's the big problem?"

Gunnar poked a finger into Phoenix's chest. "You're the problem."

Phoenix grabbed Gunnar's finger and bent it backward.

Gunnar screamed with pain and Phoenix let go. "Don't ever threaten me. Now get off this property."

"Please go," Rosie begged. "I don't understand why my life is so important to you now. You refused to let me come home or even go to my mother's funeral."

"Don't talk back to me!" her father yelled. "Heed my warning, girl. You know I don't make idle threats." With those words ringing in Rosie's ears, her father and brother walked away.

Phoenix made to go after them, but she caught his arm. "Please, just let them go."

Her nerves got the best of her, and she trembled from head to toe. Phoenix took her in his arms. "Hey, hey, they can't hurt you or me."

She buried her face in his neck, needing to feel his warmth, his strength. "But they can, Phoenix. They can hurt us. They already have."

He pulled back, his dark eyes concerned. "What do you mean?"

She stepped away, needing to be strong and away from the influence of his warmth. "Their visit reinforces everything we've been feeling for the past few weeks. Our families will never allow us to be together, to be happy. The feud will always stand between us."

"Not if we don't let it."

"You've been trying to tell your mother you're seeing me for weeks, but you haven't, and there's a reason for that. You know what her reaction is going to be, and you don't want to face that loving me will take you away from the comfort of your family. And I don't want to be the one to take you away from them, either."

"Rosie." He started to take her in his arms again, and she stepped back.

"No, we have to face this. We love each other, but that love will destroy us. We should never have gotten involved. We should've never..." A choked sob stopped her.

He stood there tall and strong, and determined. "You may want me to walk away, Rosie, but I'm not. I'm fighting for what we have and if you don't, then we never had anything."

"Your mother will never accept me and you have to

face that, Phoenix. Our families hate each other and your family will hate me, too."

"Paxton doesn't hate you, and neither does Eden. We can make this work."

"No, we can't," she said in frustration. "You're refusing to see the whole picture. My father hasn't spoken to me since the divorce, and the moment he gets wind I'm seeing you, he shows up. What does that tell you? That the feud is more important to him than I am. And he will make sure I will never see you again, and he doesn't care what he has to do to make that happen."

"Rosie, we don't have to live in Horseshoe. We can live anywhere. I can rodeo and so can you. We can make our own living, our own lives away from the influences of our families and the feud."

"And how long would it be before you hated me for taking you away from the family you love?" She held up her hand as he opened his mouth to speak. "Don't say you won't miss your family. You're a close-knit, happy group, and you will miss them. You will miss your life on Rebel Ranch. It's Jake's birthright, and he should be raised there."

His eyes narrowed on her face. "You're sounding as if this is the end of us."

She took a deep breath to gain the strength for what she had to say. "It is."

"Rosie."

She wiped away an errant tear. "Please don't make this any harder than it already is. You brought so much into my life, and now I have to let go because…"

He took her in his arms and held her, and she didn't have the strength to resist. "It's not over, Rosie."

"You're a Rebel and I'm a McCray. There's just no

way around that, and we both know it." Dixie barked and that meant Jake was awake. "I'll get Jake and his things out of the trailer."

She kissed Jake and put on his boots and parka, trying not to think. To feel. Throwing things into the diaper bag, she bit her lip to keep from crying. She handed Jake and the diaper bag to Phoenix who stood on the step. Before he could stop her, she closed the door and locked it. That might be the coward's way out, but right now it was her only way out. She heard the sound of Phoenix's truck, and she curled up on the sofa into a ball. It was over. No more happiness. No more Phoenix. No more sunshine.

*It was over.*

# Chapter Twelve

By the time Phoenix reached Rebel Ranch, he knew what he had to do: he had to tell his mother tonight. It was after seven and her truck was at the house. He needed to ask Paxton to watch Jake for a few minutes. He wasn't letting Rosie get away. They had a future together and he had to make it happen, with or without their families' approval. Jake was asleep in the car seat, but he woke up the moment the truck stopped. Phoenix carried him inside, setting him on his feet and removing his coat.

Paxton lay on the sofa in sweatpants and a T-shirt, watching TV. Jericho was in the kitchen, eating a sandwich.

Jake took the remote control out of Paxton's hand and pointed it toward the TV.

"Phoenix. He's got the control again."

"Can't you get a remote control away from a two-year-old?"

Paxton grabbed Jake and pulled him onto the sofa, tickling him. Jake wiggled and giggled and dropped the control on the floor. "No, no, no," Jake cried.

Paxton held Jake in the crook of his arm and reached down for the control. "Now listen, kid. We're watching models. Beautiful models."

"No!" Jake said. "Bob."

"Kid, you're a pain in the…"

"Paxton."

Paxton turned on the DVD, and SpongeBob appeared. Jake clapped his hands, enthralled.

"Can you watch Jake for a few minutes?"

"Why? You know the last time I lost him, and I'm not inclined to do that again. Kids aren't my thing."

Paxton got along well with Jake. He teased and picked at him and had fun with him. But Paxton pretended it was all a pain. Kids weren't his thing, as he'd said. That was only an excuse because Paxton didn't want kids to be his thing. He and Jake were forming a connection, if only Paxton would admit it.

"I want to go over and talk to Mom for a few minutes."

"She's not home."

"I saw her truck at the house."

"She's been feeling kind of down since she had the flu. Jude, Paige and Zane took her out for dinner and then a movie to cheer her up."

"When will they be back?"

Paxton lifted an eyebrow. "What am I? A mind reader? What's so important about seeing Mom tonight?" His eyes opened wide as he connected the dots. He sat up quickly with one arm wrapped around Jake. "C'mon, Phoenix. You don't want to do that. You've only known Rosie a few weeks. Give it more time."

"I know how I feel."

"It's new and feels right to you now. But you need more time to think this through."

Paxton was holding Jake so he couldn't see the TV, and Jake was trying to look around Paxton to see Sponge-Bob. Phoenix took his son from Paxton. "There's a lot more going on. I'll tell you about it later. I have to get Jake to bed."

He gave Jake a bath, dressed him in his jammies and tucked him into his crib with his blanket, Floppy and the toy horse.

Phoenix went back into the den, trying to figure out what he needed to do. Jericho was in his chair and the TV was now on a Western. It was Jericho's choice because the TV was his—a big sixty-five-inch smart HDTV. Phoenix and Paxton were hardly ever home and when they were, they worked and didn't watch much television. If they watched anything, it was usually on their phones.

Phoenix sank into his recliner.

"What's going on?" Paxton asked, his feet on the coffee table, beer in his hand.

Phoenix told him about the McCray visit and Rosie's feelings that they didn't have a future.

"They threatened you?" Paxton asked.

"It's not about that. It's about Rosie's reaction. She doesn't think we have a future because of our families, and I can't convince her otherwise."

Paxton removed his feet from the table and leaned forward, gripping his beer bottle. "It's totally about that. We've worked hard all year to get to Vegas. If the McCrays beat the crap out of you, you won't be riding, and everything we've worked for will be gone. Is that even sinking into your head?"

Phoenix had thought about a lot of things, but he hadn't even really considered that the McCrays might hurt him. He ran his hands over his face. So much was at stake. But all he could feel was the pain of losing Rosie. Nothing else mattered. His thinking might be off, but his heart was steady like a compass leading him back to

Rosie. Everything else would fall into place. That might have been naive. But then, in the last few weeks he'd gone from being a carefree cowboy to a responsible father and a man deeply in love with a woman he wanted to spend the rest of his life with. If that was daydreaming, he wanted to dream for the rest of his life.

"Phoenix, are you listening to me?"

"Yeah." He rubbed his hands together. "I don't understand why Rosie and I have to suffer because of this feud that's been going on for too many years."

"C'mon on, Phoenix. Take a break from Rosie for a few days. Let your mind clear and enjoy being home on the ranch. Three days is all you need. Three days to get your head straight. Once you tell Mom, there won't be enough mops in this country to clean up the mess."

Jericho got up and went into the kitchen. He never joined in on family squabbles or offered an opinion when it wasn't wanted.

"Jericho, do you understand how I feel?" Phoenix needed an honest answer, and he knew he would get one from Jericho.

The man poured another glass of tea. That's all Jericho ever drank—tea and water. He never touched beer or the hard stuff. In his other life, before he came to the ranch, he said he'd had too much of the bad stuff, and he never wanted to go back to being a man out of control.

Leaning against the counter, Rico said, "Miss Kate is a fair woman, but when it comes to the McCrays, her stance is clear and everyone knows it. There's no middle ground for her. The McCrays are off-limits. I've heard it said that some men give up everything for true love. You have to ask yourself how much you're willing to sacrifice for the love you feel. What can you live with or without?

It won't be easy, and as surely as the sun comes up tomorrow, you'll feel pain like you've never felt before. Just be sure you're willing to go through that." He walked into his bedroom without another word.

For the first time, Phoenix knew the love he had for Rosie would be tested in ways he'd never considered. His mother was not going to allow Rosie into the family. And Phoenix had to decide if he could live away from the ranch and away from the Rebels.

He got up and walked toward his bedroom. After a shower, he sat on the edge of his bed, staring at his phone. He wanted to call Rosie so bad it hurt. But he knew she wouldn't answer. Instead he sent a text: Call me when you're ready to talk. I'll be waiting. He meant every word. There was no middle ground for him, either. His future was with Rosie, and it would take a part of him to walk away from this ranch and his family. But somewhere inside him, he would find the strength.

ABOUT FIVE THE next morning, Jake crawled into bed with him. Phoenix pulled him close and covered them with a blanket. He kissed the top of his son's head. This was what was important. His son. Rosie. And their life. It was clear to him now. Nothing mattered without her.

The next time he woke up, he could hear Paxton and Rico in the kitchen, cooking breakfast. He changed Jake's diaper, dressed him and slipped socks on his feet. Jake ran to the kitchen and crawled into his high chair. Phoenix locked the tray in place and went to fill a sippy cup with milk.

His thoughts inward, he sat at the table with Paxton and Rico, eating scrambled eggs, bacon and biscuits.

"Rico, Elias and I are checking the herds this morning," Paxton said around a mouthful of scrambled eggs. "Why don't you and Jake come with us? It's Saturday, and not much is going on except just taking care of stuff."

Phoenix wiped his mouth on a paper napkin. "I'm going to talk to Mom this morning."

Paxton slammed his fork into his plate. "Why can't you let this go?"

At Paxton's loud voice, tears filled Jake's eyes, and he reached out his arms to Phoenix. "Dad-dy."

"It's okay, son." Phoenix wiped Jake's mouth, removed his plate and cup from the tray and took him out of the high chair. "Uncle Paxton's being silly."

Jake ran to Paxton and slapped his arm. "No!" He darted to the sofa and jumped on it. Paxton was fast on his heels and grabbed Jake, tickling him until the house was filled with giggly screams.

Rico reached for his hat. "I'm going to the office to talk to Falcon. I'll see you later."

Paxton jumped up. "Hey, I'm coming with you." He grabbed his hat and headed for the door, looking back at Jake on the sofa. "You want to come with us?"

Jake slipped from the sofa and looked at Paxton and then at Phoenix. He shook his head and ran to his father. Phoenix was hoping Jake would go so he he'd have time to talk to his mother, but it was too soon. Jake wasn't comfortable anywhere without Phoenix.

After Rico and Paxton left, Jake played with his toys and Phoenix did the dishes. He laid the dish towel on the counter and turned to see Jake wasn't in the den. Had he gotten out when Phoenix wasn't looking?

"Jake," he called, running to the front door to see that it was still closed.

Jake came out of the bedroom, trying to put on his

jacket. He was trying to poke one arm through the hood part, and the other arm was in an armhole. "Momma," he muttered.

Phoenix took the coat from him. "Not right now, son." How was he going to tell Jake they weren't going to see Rosie today? It was their routine and Jake was into a routine. Now he had to break his son's heart, just like Phoenix's was breaking.

"No." Jake tried to grab the jacket back.

"Stop it." Phoenix pointed a finger at Jake's face. Jake's bottom lip trembled, and Phoenix picked him up and hugged him. "Time for Bob." He turned on the TV, and Jake curled up on a pillow Paxton had left on the sofa. It wasn't the best parenting, but it would work for now, until he figured out how to deal with the next few hours.

His phone buzzed, and he hurried to find it. It was on the nightstand where he'd left it last night after texting Rosie. Glancing at the caller ID, he saw it was Ms. Henshaw. He had no idea why she would be calling. Maybe she had to make another routine check or something. He clicked on.

"I have some bad news, Mr. Rebel."

A knot formed in his stomach, and he walked into the den so he could see Jake. "What is it?"

"Valerie Green has surfaced."

The knot tightened. "And?" He knew there was a big *and* coming.

"A judge in Colorado ruled that her maternal rights were illegally terminated."

Phoenix sank into a chair. "What?"

"The judge has ordered another hearing for custody of Jake."

"No! They can't do this. He's my son and they just can't do this."

"It's already been done, Mr. Rebel. I'm so sorry. I got a call at home, and I'm in my office this morning because I felt you deserved a personal call. And I have to meet with the CPS worker handling the case."

"Valerie abandoned him. How can they say her rights were terminated illegally?"

"She contends that she's been calling her grandmother regularly, and her phone records back it up. Her husband is in a high-powered job in the military, and they've been stationed in several war-torn countries. She felt it was best if Jake stayed with her grandmother. It seems she didn't just abandon him as the neighbor and the girlfriend had said. She got a judge to listen to her, and now another judge will rule on who gets custody of Jake."

The walls caved in on Phoenix, and he felt the pain rip though him. He had trouble breathing. He had trouble thinking. He glanced at Jake lying on the sofa, his eyes on the TV screen, totally enraptured. Now Jake's world would be torn apart once again. So would Phoenix's.

He swallowed the lump in his throat. "When is this hearing?"

"That's the main reason I'm calling. Since Jake now resides in Texas, the Colorado judge ruled the hearing to be held in Austin at ten o'clock on Monday. Ms. Green had it rushed through because she wants her son. And the judge agreed with her. By the way, she's now Mrs. Stephens."

Phoenix stood, his back straight and his resolve strong. "She will not get my son. I don't care who she is or what she contends. Jake belongs with me. I will fight this with everything I have."

"I'm so sorry, Mr. Rebel. I have more bad news."

He gripped his phone so hard he was waiting for it to crumble in his hand. "What else could there be?"

"The judge has ordered that Jake be removed from your custody until after the hearing."

"No! No way. Jake stays with me!"

"Mr. Rebel, you have to abide by the court's ruling. It's just two days."

"No way in hell are they taking my son. He's been through enough. The judge should have the decency to leave him where he is until after the hearing. Why uproot him now? They did that once. Are they even thinking about Jake and what this will do to him?"

"Yes, they are. The judge feels Mrs. Stephens has a right to visit with her son before the hearing."

Phoenix gritted his teeth and wanted to scream. To Phoenix, Valerie had no rights. He took a deep breath to calm himself. "Ms. Henshaw, please, don't let them take my son."

"It's out of my hands now. Just be patient. The judge will go over everything and you will have a chance to put your case forward, as will Mrs. Stephens. The best parent will get custody. Trust me on that. In the meantime, Jake will be put with a very nice foster family, and Mrs. Stephens will visit with him later today and on Sunday. We have to go by the rules, Mr. Rebel."

"They're going to take Jake today?"

"Yes. That's why I'm calling on a Saturday."

Phoenix ended the call abruptly, slipped his phone into his pocket and went into the bedroom. He started throwing things into a diaper bag—everything he and Jake would need for the next few days. If they left now, they could be out of the state in no time. The authorities

would never find them. That was his only option. He had
to run. To keep his son, he had to run.

Pulling jeans and shirts out of his closet, he paused.
If he kidnapped his son—and that was what he would
be doing—he would be wanted for the rest of his life by
the police. No family. No rodeo. No Rosie. That was no
life. That was pure hell. He couldn't put Jake through
that. He sat on the bed and sucked air into his tight lungs.
They were going to take his son. How could he let them
do that?

Jake trailed in, dragging his coat behind him. "Momma,
Dad-dy."

He picked him up and kissed his cheek. "I love you,
son. In the next few hours we have to be strong. Can you
be strong?"

Holding his son against him, he knew he couldn't run
with Jake. They had to do it the legal way. Even though
it would take a slice of his heart to let go, he had to believe he could get his son back. He had to call Gabe, his
uncle, who was a lawyer and could help him.

A knock sounded at the door. With more strength than
he'd thought he had, he got to his feet and made his way
into the den with Jake in his arms. Through the glass on
the door, he could see a woman and an officer outside.
His mom, Grandpa and his brothers stood behind them.
Evidently CPS had been looking for him at the house.

He took a deep breath and opened the door.

"Mr. Phoenix Rebel?" the woman asked.

"Yes."

"I'm Vera Connors with Child Protective Services.
I have a court order to remove minor child Jake Rebel
from your custody temporarily."

*No way on this earth!* was his first thought. But with

the maturity he'd learned over the last few weeks, he stood tall and looked the woman right in the eyes. "He's two years old. He's not going to understand what's happening. All he'll know is that you're taking him away from me. How can I explain that to him?"

"Mr. Rebel, I understand your situation, but kids are very resilient and have a short memory. Jake will do fine."

Even at that young age, Jake sensed what was going on, and he wrapped his arms around Phoenix's neck and burrowed into his chest.

Ms. Connors attempted to take Jake from him, but Jake slapped her hand and shouted, "No!" and burrowed further into Phoenix.

"Can't you see this is upsetting him?"

Ms. Connors motioned to the officer, who physically removed Jake from Phoenix's arms. Phoenix wanted to hit him, but he curled his hands into fists to prevent that. Jake screamed and kicked and shouted, "No. No. No!" The man walked out with Jake screaming at the top of his lungs. "Dad-dy," Jake screamed, holding his arms out toward Phoenix.

His chest hurt and his breath came in gasps. Ms. Connors handed him some papers, and then she followed the officer. Jake's screams of "Dad-dy!" echoed through the landscape, and the family stood there paralyzed with anger, just as Phoenix was. He put his hands over his ears to stop the sound. He'd never felt so powerless in his life. He couldn't protect his own child.

*They'd taken his son.*

# Chapter Thirteen

Phoenix's brothers, his mom and Grandpa gathered around him. His mom hugged him. Grandpa patted his arm and Quincy rubbed his shoulder.

"You'll get him back," Quincy said. "Just stay calm."

*Calm!*

He'd been sinking into a dark abyss, and nothing or no one could reach him. That one word jolted him and ignited fire in his belly. How could he be calm when they'd just taken his child?

He stared at Quincy. "You want me to be calm? Would you be calm if someone had ripped your child from your arms?" He looked at Falcon. "How about you? Would you be calm if someone had taken John?" He glanced at Egan. "Would you be calm if someone had stolen Justin?" His eyes settled on Jude. "Would you be calm if someone had snatched Zane?"

They looked back at him with worried expressions.

Jude stepped closer to him. "Quincy didn't mean it like that, Phoenix. We know how you're feeling and we just want to help."

"You don't know how I'm feeling, Jude. No one knows because you haven't had your child taken from you, so don't try to be sympathetic or consoling. I don't need it. I just need my kid."

His mom put an arm around his waist. "Son…"

He stepped back. "I'm sorry…I'm losing it. I didn't mean to…"

His brothers gathered round, and for a moment he leaned on them for support because they were family and he needed…he needed…

Turning, he went into his room and closed the door. Sitting on the bed, he buried his face in his hands. *Daddy* ran through his mind like a chant he was never going to escape. He would hear it for the rest of his life. He took a couple of deep breaths to keep the tears at bay. He wouldn't cry. His dad had always said strong men didn't cry. A Rebel didn't cry. He'd been wrong.

There was only one person who could help him. He reached in his pocket and pulled out his phone. He touched the screen a couple times and waited for her to answer. She didn't. He knew she wasn't going to click on, but he had to try. When it went to voice mail, he left a message. "Rosie, please pick up. I need you. Something bad has happened, and I need to talk to you. Please call me." Tears clogged his throat, and he had to click off.

She'd call. He'd just have to wait. In the meantime, he had to find a way to get his son back. He called Gabe only to learn that his mother had already contacted him. Phoenix got to his feet, reached for his hat and headed for the door to meet Gabe at his office. He stopped when he noticed Jake's coat on the floor. He picked it up. They had taken him without a jacket or any of his things. What kind of agency would do that?

He reached for the diaper bag he'd stuffed earlier. He removed most of it and added Jake's blanket, his jacket,

Floppy, the horse, some clothes, diapers and a sippy cup. He slipped it over his shoulder and carried it into the den. Everyone looked anxiously at him as if they didn't know what to say to him. And they had reason to be cautious. He was teetering on the brink of a total breakdown. But he was stronger than that.

"Where are you going?" his mom asked.

"To see Gabe and to take these things to Ms. Henshaw so she can give them to Jake. He'll feel better if he has his familiar stuff."

"It'll work out, son. Just have faith."

He took a couple steps toward the door and realized this was the time he had to make a stand. For his future. For Jake's future. He turned to face his mother.

"I love you, Mom, but I've been avoiding telling you something because I know you're not going to like it."

His mom waved a hand. "Go see Gabe and we can talk later. I'm sure it's nothing important."

"It is. To me. You've asked about Rosie and I avoided the question, as did everyone else, and there's a reason for that. Rosie is Rosemary... McCray Wilcott."

"No!" She covered her mouth with her hand.

"Yes. I love her and Jake loves her. I'm planning a future with her if I can convince her to marry me."

"No." His mom shook her head. "I forbid it. You will stay away from that girl. Do you hear me, Phoenix?"

"Mom..." Quincy put an arm around their mother's shoulder.

"Stay out of this, Quincy." Their mother shook off Quincy's arm.

"It's okay," Phoenix said to Quincy. "I knew this was how she would react. That's okay, too. Mom has a right to feel the way she does, but if you remember, I was one of the boys who was shot. If I can forgive, Mom, I was hoping you could, too. If not, after I see Gabe, I'll come back and clear out my stuff."

"No!" his mom screamed after him. "Come back here, Phoenix."

He kept walking with Quincy, Falcon and Jude fast on his heels. He climbed into his truck, and Quincy yanked open the door.

"Phoenix, you can't drop a bombshell like that and just leave. We have to talk this through for Mom's sake."

"I'm through talking, Quincy. I have the fight of my life on my hands, and that's all that's on my mind right now."

"You need your family to get through this."

"I need Rosie, Quincy. That's who I need. I'm sorry this hurts Mom, but it's hurting me, too. I was hoping I wouldn't have to choose…"

"Phoenix—" Jude tried to get a word in, but Grandpa pushed him aside.

"This is your home, boy, and you're always welcome here. Don't you ever forget that. You go get that little whippersnapper back and we'll all be waiting. That's what families do and we're all family. Just don't cut those ties forever, because no one here wants that, especially your mother." Grandpa patted his shoulder, and words clogged Phoenix's throat. He only nodded and pulled the door closed. As he backed out, Paxton jumped into the passenger side.

Phoenix stopped the truck. "Get out."

"Hey. I always ride shotgun."

"Not today."

"C'mon, Phoenix. We shared a lot over the years, and

you're going to need someone today. I'm here, so let's don't argue about it."

"Thanks, Pax, but Rosie is the only person I need to get through this. As soon as I talk to Gabe, I'm going to find her, because I can't get through this without her."

"Man, you really love her, don't you?"

"Yes. I really do."

Paxton slid out of the truck. "Call if you need me."

Phoenix drove away, resisting the urge to look back at the ranch he'd loved all his life. But like Rico had said, he had to make a choice, and he made the one that was right for him.

ROSIE WOKE UP to barking. Sitting up, she realized she was still on the sofa in her clothes. She'd cried herself to sleep, and Dixie was having an antsy fit to go outside and pee. Rosie got up and opened the door, and Dixie darted out.

After making coffee, she let Dixie back in. It was cold outside. She opened the refrigerator and saw Phoenix's orange juice, and all her love for him brought tears to her eyes. How was she going to go on without him and Jake?

On the floor was a toy horse. She picked it up and slid into the booth. She knew without a doubt that her father had meant every word he'd said about hurting Phoenix. She couldn't let that happen, even if it meant giving Phoenix up. A sob rose in her throat, and she noticed her phone on the table. She clicked on and read Phoenix's message.

Touching the screen, she muttered, "Oh, Phoenix, don't do this. It isn't easy, but we have to stay apart. It's for the best." She had a voice mail from him, too. She didn't listen to it. It was just too hard. Turning her phone off, she held it for a moment, as if she could feel Phoenix's presence, and then she went to take a shower and get dressed for the day. She had to make decisions and she needed a clear head, even though her heart was breaking.

By midmorning she knew she had to leave the trailer because Phoenix would come back. He wouldn't give up. He wouldn't be the man she loved if he did. After practicing with Lady and making sure the horses had enough feed, she headed out for she knew not where, but a few days would give her a better perspective. She didn't have a rodeo this weekend, so she would just take a break. Just her and Dixie.

PHOENIX MADE IT to Gabe's office, which was on the square in Horseshoe, in record time. The receptionist's office was empty, and he walked through to a bigger office. Gabe was on the phone.

Gabe was his mother's baby brother and her only brother. Phoenix's grandmother had died when Gabe was fourteen years old, and he'd come to live with the Rebel family. He'd grown up with the Rebel boys, and he favored them, too, with dark eyes and hair. As soon as he graduated from high school, he was off to college and a law career, but part of Gabe would always be a cowboy.

He waved Phoenix to a leather chair in front of his desk. After a moment, he clicked off his phone. "Do you have some papers for me?" Gabe got down to business and Phoenix was grateful for that. He wasn't in a mood to talk about family.

Phoenix handed him the papers Ms. Connors had given him and the file Phoenix had brought from Denver. Gabe quickly went through them. "Tell me all you know."

Phoenix went over everything that had happened since he'd found out he was Jake's father.

"So everyone the police investigated at the time said that Ms. Green Stephens had abandoned Jake?"

"Yes. That's why I was granted full custody, but now she's saying she was in contact with the grandmother at all times."

Gabe went through the papers again. "I have a lot of checking to do, and since it's Saturday I may not get the answers I want, but I know a good detective who can pull answers out of thin air. But again, it's Saturday, and he has a family, so this is going to be slow go."

"The hearing is Monday, Gabe. We don't have time to go slow."

"Mmm. I wonder how Ms. Green Stephens got this pushed through so fast and what's her hurry."

"I have no idea, but Jake was so upset when they took him. I have to get him back, Gabe. Do whatever you can and then some."

"I'm on it, but Lacey's three weeks away from delivery, and I can't get too far away from home because I want to be there with the twins are born."

Gabe's wife was expecting a boy and a girl, and the family was happy for them. Gabe had lost his first son in an ATV accident and the family thought he would never recover, but he'd found Lacey and fallen in love. He'd adopted Lacey's half sister, and they'd become a family.

"The hearing's on Monday so you should be safe."

Gabe leaned back in his chair. "That's just the problem, Phoenix. I don't have enough time to prepare this case or enough evidence to discredit what Ms. Green is saying. I have to ask for a continuance, but at this late date I'm not sure a judge is going to grant it."

"No continuance, Gabe. I want Jake in my custody as soon as possible."

Gabe leaned forward, his hands folded on the desk. "I have to be honest, Phoenix. This woman wants her child and she's not leaving any room for error. The judge in Colorado is on her side. That's why this has been pushed through so fast. Evidently he saw that something was done illegally, and he wants it corrected in the mother's favor."

Phoenix got to his feet. "She can't do this. She left him with her sixty-six-year-old grandmother. How can they see any right in that? She hasn't seen him in two years. He doesn't know who she is." He poked a finger into his chest. "He knows who *I* am. He knows I'm his daddy."

"Just calm down."

"I wish everyone would stop telling me to calm down. This woman has had my child removed from my care. Jake was screaming his head off calling for me, and I'll never get that sound out of my head."

Gabe stared at him. "Is this the same Phoenix who spiked the punch at parties just for laughs, put itch powder in my boots and pulled just about every trick in the book on all of us at one time or another?"

"I grew up the moment I learned I was a father."

"I can see that." Gabe opened the folder Phoenix had given him. "I'm going to call Levi Coyote..."

"Who?"

"He's the PI I was telling you about. He used to be a cop in Austin and now works for the DA's office and takes a few private cases. He's a good investigator. If Valerie Green has anything in her past she's trying to hide, he will find it. Just be prepared for the results."

"What do you mean?"

Gabe looked at him, and Phoenix's nerves tightened.

He knew something bad was coming by the dark look in his uncle's eyes. "She is the mother, and in the majority of custody cases involving a baby, a judge will grant the mother custody unless she has a criminal record or is seen as unfit. You need to prepare yourself for that."

"I'll never be able to accept that. Jake belongs with me. I know that. I only knew Valerie for a little while, but I know she's not a better parent than me. I would never leave my son with someone else for two years. To me that is unforgivable. That's not a parent."

"I'll start making calls. I'm hoping Levi will be on board with this." He glanced at Phoenix. "You go home and talk to your mother and wait for me to call you."

"You've talked to Mom about Rosie?"

"Yes, she's very upset. Dating a McCray?" Gabe shook his head. "That's like asking your mom to cozy up to a rattlesnake. You're her baby and she's not letting go easily. Go make peace and I'll sort through all of this."

"I can't do that. I have somewhere else I need to go, and Mom already knows my decision."

"Phoenix…"

He held up a hand. "I already heard it all from my brothers. I'm making decisions for my future and what's right for me. I'm sorry my mom doesn't agree. But I love Rosemary McCray, and I plan to marry her one way or another."

He walked out the door to his truck. Once inside, he called Ms. Henshaw's number. It went to voice mail and he asked her to call him back. Then he headed for Rosie's.

As he crossed the cattle guard, he noticed Rosie's truck was gone. He went around back and everything was quiet, except for the occasional neighing of the horses.

A fresh roll of hay was in the corral, the automatic

feeder was on and the barn door was open so the horses could get inside when they wanted. All signs Rosie had left and wasn't planning on coming back anytime soon. But he could be wrong. He'd wait just in case.

He looked toward the trailer where Rosie lived, and then to the water trough where she bathed because she loved baths. He planned to build her a house with the biggest tub he could find. She would never have to bathe in a water trough again.

His cell dinged. He pulled it out and sat in a lawn chair they used in the yard when they watched Jake play with Dixie. It was a text from Gabe: Levi's on the case. More later. Phoenix quickly texted back with a thank you.

The cold north wind whipped around him, but he didn't feel it. This was where he'd found happiness with Rosie. It was their private little world where hate and bitterness weren't allowed. Only love that was now being tested by the strongest force there was—feuding families who could tear them apart.

He sat in the chair feeling lonelier than he ever had in his whole life. He'd always had family around him, a supportive, loving family. Now he was alone, fighting for a woman he loved and a son who was his. He didn't know if he could win this battle, but he would keep trying. He'd always heard that love worked miracles. He desperately needed a miracle.

He didn't know how long he sat there listening to the wind howl and watching the leaves dance in the breeze. The chill finally reached him, and he got up and walked to his truck. He slipped on his all-weather jacket and climbed inside. Sighing, he opened the glove compartment and pulled out their marriage license. With it in his hand, he soon fell asleep, and the buzz of his phone woke him.

Hoping it was Rosie, he hurriedly clicked on. It was Ms. Henshaw. "I'm returning your call, Mr. Rebel?"

"They took Jake without his favorite stuffed animal, his blanket, his jacket or his shoes. I have his things and I was hoping you could take them to him. They would make him more comfortable."

"As I've been told, they had to get the baby out as quickly as possible because you were resisting and they did what they had to at the time."

"They jerked my kid out of my arms. What did they expect me to do? Hand him over without any emotions?"

"I know this is hard on you, but please be patient. The worst is yet to come. A judge will decide if Jake belongs with you or with his mother. You'll have to face that."

He gritted his teeth. "Jake was so upset and I'm worried about him."

"Babies adjust quickly, and I'm sure Jake is fine. Once he gets with other kids and toys he'll settle down."

"Have you spoken with Ms. Connors?"

"No, and I'm sure she would've called if anything was wrong with Jake. Trust me, he's playing with kids and having fun. You don't have to worry."

"Oh, but I do worry, Ms. Henshaw. Jake had better be fine or you haven't heard the last of me." He laid his phone in the console and took a moment to cool down.

A spotlight Rosie had installed on the property came on, distracting him. How long had he been sitting here? Picking up his phone again, he checked to see if Gabe had left any more messages. He hadn't. That wasn't good.

He looked at the trailer. Rosie wasn't coming home tonight. Once again, he called her and left a long message about what had happened and told her how much he loved her. Afterward he slipped the marriage license back into the glove compartment.

*Rosie, please come home.*

## Chapter Fourteen

Rosie drove and drove with no destination in mind. Dixie sat on the passenger side, staring out the window, barking occasionally at something that caught her eye. Rosie stopped in Gruene, Texas, a small town between Austin and San Antonio, located near the Guadalupe River. She'd been through here many times but had never visited. It boasted of having the oldest dance hall in Texas. Not that she was planning on dancing, but the little town looked interesting.

She spent the day strolling through quaint antiques and specialty shops and eating barbeque in a small diner all by herself. It was lonely. For the first time she really knew what lonely was. She'd only thought she did before. There was a hole in her now that couldn't be filled by anyone but Phoenix and Jake.

After walking until her legs hurt, she decided to spend the night and rented a room in a Victorian cottage. It was a historical home and it was lovely, even though she had to share a bath with another couple. At least she had a bathtub, and the other couple was out. She took advantage of it. She soaked in the claw-foot tub, thinking about her life and what she was going to do now.

Tears rolled from her eyes. She needed a good cry, so

she made no effort to stop them. Dixie whined on the rug on the floor and Rosie ignored her. She hated to have run out on Phoenix like that, but she needed time. The time was painful without him, though. She had to make a big decision: Could she live without Phoenix?

Afterward she scrubbed her face, trying to erase the telltale signs of her meltdown. She then wrapped a towel around herself, scurried to her room and curled up on the bed. It was dark outside now and she didn't turn on the light. She didn't need it. Darkness was the blanket that covered her heart and soul, and by morning she would know what she had to do.

With or without Phoenix.

PHOENIX SLEPT IN his truck at Rosie's until about two that morning. He then drove home and fell into bed, exhausted beyond anything he'd ever felt. Rosie was gone and they'd taken his son. There was just no way to put a Band-Aid on a hurt that big. He slept restlessly with *Dad-dy* running through his mind like bits and pieces of a sad lullaby. He got up at five and stared at the empty crib. This was about the time Jake would crawl into bed with him. What must be going through his little mind now that his daddy wasn't there? There would be no one to comfort him like Phoenix had. No one loved him like Phoenix, except maybe Rosie. Filled with renewed anger, he went to take a shower and then changed and got dressed for the day.

He'd checked his phone first thing, and there had been no word from Rosie or Gabe. That bothered him, and he planned to call Gabe by seven. But first, he sat on his bed and left Rosie another message. He couldn't understand why she wasn't calling him back. Their goodbye wasn't final. Not to him. She just had to call him. Obviously she wasn't reading his messages or she would have called about Jake. He knew that beyond any doubt.

Hearing noises in the kitchen, he went to join Paxton and Jericho.

"Hey." Paxton seemed startled to see him. "Jericho's making pancakes. Have a seat."

"I don't have time. I…"

Jericho blocked the door. For a big man, he moved fast. "When was the last time you ate?"

"I don't know. I have to go into town to see Gabe."

"It's not even six in the morning. Eat breakfast and then go."

The smell of bacon made him aware that he was hungry and that he hadn't eaten since yesterday morning.

Paxton threw an arm around Phoenix's shoulders. "Fill the tank and you'll be ready to go all day."

Pax was right. He needed strength to get through this. He turned back to the table and noticed his orange juice was waiting for him. He sat down and took a big swig, and the tight nerves that had him bound in a vise eased for a moment.

"How's it going with Gabe?" Paxton asked around a mouthful of pancake.

"He has a private investigator on the case and I haven't heard from him. Since it's the weekend, he said it would be slow going, but we don't have time for slow."

"Doesn't Gabe present your side and Valerie's attorney presents hers and the judge will decide who is the better parent?"

Phoenix twisted his glass. "That's about it, but we need something to poke holes in her case. We just need more time."

"Stop worrying. Gabe's a good lawyer and he'll figure something out."

"I'm worried about Jake. It's his first morning to wake up without me." He placed his fork in his plate, losing his appetite. "And I can't find Rosie. I stayed at her place until after midnight waiting and she never showed up."

"Did you call her?"

Phoenix pushed his plate away. "Yeah. Constantly. She's turned off her phone. She's not going to jeopardize my well-being by seeing me. I just want her to know about Jake."

"Phoenix…"

He got to his feet. "I'll see y'all later." He couldn't sit there and have a normal conversation when his insides burned with anger at what had been done to his life. And to Rosie's. And to Jake's.

Before he reached the door, it opened and his mother stood there. A new kind of anger shot through him. He didn't want to deal with his mother and the feud this morning.

"Phoenix, I'm so glad you're home. We need to talk."

"I've said all I'm going to say."

"I'm fixing a big dinner for the family and we'll talk afterward. We can sort this out, but we have to talk first."

His mother hadn't heard a word he'd said. She was just focused on getting him away from Rosie.

"I won't be home for lunch. I'm going into town to see Gabe. Jake's custody is the most important thing on my mind right now, and I can't think about anything else."

Paxton and Jericho eased past them and out the door. Cowards!

Phoenix took a deep breath and knew he had to talk to his mother. He owed her that. "We can talk now."

He sat in his recliner and his mother sat on the sofa. He wasn't sure where to start. He thought of all the years his mother had loved and supported him and taken up for him when he'd done something wrong. He was never punished. He was the favorite son. He was her baby. And it would be so hard to break her heart. But the mature Phoenix knew there was no other way.

"I didn't mean to fall in love with Rosie. I've seen her at the rodeos many times and I wasn't actually avoiding her. We just never interacted because of the feud. Then one day she took up two spaces parking her trailer and it irritated me and I told her so. We had words, and I felt bad afterward because I was rude to her. I wanted to apologize, but I let it go—because of the feud. Then I found out I was a father and I went shopping for baby things and there she was. It was like fate that she was in the same store at the same time I was. I had the chance to apologize for my behavior and we agreed to call a truce. She helped me pick out things for Jake. But we both agreed that was the end of it."

"It should have been the end of it," his mother said in a tone of voice he'd heard many times over the years. The strong, determined voice that said she wasn't taking any crap from her sons.

"Yeah." He rubbed his hands together. "But fate stepped in once again. There was something about Rosie that drew me. I've been with a lot of girls over the years and not one of them ever touched my heart. It was always just fun. But with Rosie it was different. I wanted to know more about her. I didn't remember her from school like all the other McCray kids."

"Are you saying you pursued her?"

"Yes, ma'am. I did. And she was angry, very angry

at me for invading her privacy. She told me to leave. But I wanted her to see my kid. The little boy she'd helped pick out the baby stuff for. That did the trick. Jake stole her heart just like she stole mine. I know you don't want to hear that."

"Son, you've only known her a few weeks."

"It took a moment to fall in love." He snapped his fingers. "Just like that. The moment I looked at the fire in her blue eyes, I knew I wanted to see that fire for the rest of my life." He glanced at his mom and saw the hurt in her eyes and did his best to ignore it. "I love Rosie. It's complicated to describe, yet it's simple to me."

"I want you to stop seeing her." The words were spoken softly but lined with the power of steel.

He'd never gone against his mother in his whole life. Today he would have to be stronger than he'd ever been. Because standing up to his mom would require a man where a young boy used to be.

He rubbed his hands together until they were numb. "I've watched you grieve for Dad since the day he died. If I have to give up Rosie, I'll grieve for her for the rest of mine. Is that the kind of life you want for me—one filled with sadness?" He stared directly at her.

She scooted closer to him. "Son…"

"You don't even know her. She's a warm, loving, giving person, and Jake took to her right away. Just like I did. Ira married her off to an older man who beat and abused her for over a year. He finally beat her so bad she lost her child. She's like a broken doll, Mom. I've never felt as deeply as I have for anyone like I do for her. It's like we need each other to be whole. Dad said a Rebel man loves forever, and I now know what he was talking about."

"You just feel sorry for this girl. Give yourself time and you'll get over her. It's just an infatuation, Phoenix."

He stood, growing tired of beating his head against a brick wall. "It's not an infatuation. It's the real thing, and I'm sorry it hurts you. But it might not be too much to worry about, because Rosie broke up with me. You see, Ira threatened to hurt me if she didn't stop seeing me, and she doesn't want any harm to come to me. That's the type of person she is."

"What? That man threatened you?"

Phoenix shook his head. "It doesn't matter anymore. I have to go to get my son back, and then I'll find Rosie. I'm sorry." He reached down and kissed her cheek, and a tear slipped from her eye. He braced himself against the pain he was causing her and walked out the door.

ROSIE TOSSED AND turned and was unable to sleep. Dixie yelped at her a couple times for disturbing her sleep. In the early hours of the morning, she fell into a deep sleep, and when she woke up, she knew what she had to do. There was no other choice for her.

She dressed and had the breakfast the inn provided and then she was on her way home. Her phone was in the bottom of her purse and she was tempted to look at it, but that would be torture, reading his messages and not able to answer—just yet.

As she drove, a plan formed in her mind. To go forward with her life, it was very clear she had to face her father and explain how she felt about what he'd done to her life and tell him he couldn't control her anymore. Somewhere during the night she'd found her strength. She wasn't going back to being that young girl who'd been manipulated and abused. Adversity had made her stronger. She'd just lost track of that, thinking about her father hurting Phoenix. That was the last thing she wanted, and she was going to make sure it never happened.

First she went home to check on her horses and the trailer. Everything was fine. There was a nip in the air and the horses were feisty, galloping around the corral, kicking up their heels. She threw a saddle over Lady and raced her around the barrels she had set up. Exercise was what Lady needed.

After exercising all three horses, she took a shower and dressed again, this time more carefully. She braided her hair to keep it out of her face. She didn't need any distractions for the task ahead of her. Then she was off to Horseshoe.

As a safety measure, she stopped in at the sheriff's office and spoke to Wyatt Carson before making the trip out to the McCray ranch. It had been ten years since she'd been home. She remembered the day vividly. Her wedding was in Austin and she and her mother had driven in early. Her father and brothers had come later. She'd tried to talk to her mother but was told she had to do what her father wanted. And that was that.

After the wedding, Derek wouldn't allow her to go home. He said her family could visit her in their home, and once again she was controlled by a man. When the divorce was final, she vowed she'd never be controlled by a man again.

She took the winding dirt road that led to the two-story house back in the woods. It once had been a beautiful Victorian house with a wide veranda in the front, but with no money the house had been in disrepair when she'd left. She was happy to see the house had been painted and looked like it had in her childhood. There were even rosebushes in the flowerbeds, her mother's favorite. Someone had been keeping them up.

A double-wide trailer was set off to the left, Malachi and his wife Cheryl's house. Two more trailers were back in the woods, and she assumed they belonged to her brothers Axel and Anson.

It was after lunch and trucks were parked by the garage, so she knew her father was home, and probably Gunnar, too. He and his wife lived in the house also. But Cindy had left Gunnar years ago, and Rosie didn't know if she was back or not.

Chickens pecked in the yard, and she noticed goats in a pen. In the distance, beyond the corrals and barn, cows munched on grass. If anything good had come out of her marriage, and she was still doubtful of that, the McCray ranch had been saved, and the family could now make a living from it.

Taking a deep breath, she stroked Dixie, picked up an old newspaper she'd brought from the dash and got out of the truck. She walked up the steps with butterflies in her stomach, but wasn't backing out now. This was too important.

She knocked on the door, and it was opened almost immediately by Cindy. A different, older Cindy. Her dark blond hair was pulled back into a ponytail, and she wiped her hands on a dish towel. Cindy had left because she was tired of being used as a maid and she was tired of being hit. Cindy deserved better than that, and Rosie hoped things were better now. But, then, Rosie tended to believe in fairy tales. Occasionally.

"Rosie? Is that you?"

"Hi, Cindy. I'd like to speak with my father."

"My, aren't you all formal and all." She nodded over

her shoulder. "The guys are in the kitchen finishing lunch. It's Sunday so things are slow around here." She leaned in close and whispered, "Are you sure you want to be here?"

Before she could answer, her father and her brothers Gunnar and Malachi came into the living room and saw her at the front door. She walked past Cindy to face them.

"What are you doing here, girl?" her father demanded.

Her nerves tingled with anticipation and fear. "I have something to say and I'm going to say it."

Her father sat in his recliner as if she wasn't there, and then he looked at her with the coldest glance she'd ever seen. "You disgraced this family and you have the nerve to come here and face us."

That one sentence obliterated all the shaky nerves inside her. "And you have the nerve to come to my trailer and tell me who I can and cannot see."

"You'd better leave, girl. You're not welcome here."

"You sold me off to Derek Wilcott like a prized heifer, and he beat and abused me almost every day of the time I spent with him. He beat me so severely the last time that he killed my child. That's why he went to prison. That's what you did to your daughter, and you still can look me in the eye and say those cruel words to me."

"That's all in your head. Derek said you fell down the stairs and lost the baby, and he went to prison because the judge believed you and not him."

"Did you bother to come to the trial or check the records or ask anyone for the truth?"

"There was no need."

"I guess not if you don't care anything for the daughter who went through hell to save this ranch." She looked around at the new curtains and furniture. "I see you've used the money well."

"I think you'd better leave," Gunnar said.

Rosie ignored him, walked over and laid the newspaper she'd saved from the trial in her father's lap. "Read it. The truth is in there, the real truth, if you're interested."

He made no move to look at it.

"I sent you almost every dime I received from my divorce, and your response was to disown me and not to allow me at my own mother's funeral. But I came anyway. After all the cars had left the cemetery, I sat with her for a long time and cried because she was the only one who cared anything about me. When I was in the hospital from the beating, she came. Did you know that?"

Her father didn't look at her or respond.

"She came every day I was in the hospital, and she gave me money to rent an apartment so I wouldn't have to go back to that house. Did you know that?"

"Where would she get money to do that?"

"She said she'd saved it from the grocery money, because there were days she thought about leaving and she wanted to be able to do it if she ever had the nerve."

Her father's sun-browned skin turned pale.

"But she stayed. God bless her, she stayed through it all, but she never forgot her baby daughter. She gave me the strength to get back up on my feet and make a life for myself."

"You live in a horse trailer."

"But it's my trailer, paid for with money I earned. Someday I will have enough money to buy my own home because I'm working very hard to accomplish that."

Her father stared down at the newspaper in his lap.

"If that's all you have to say, you can leave now," Gunnar told her.

She glanced at her older brother. "No, that's not all I have to say. Before I came here, I went by the sheriff's office and told him you threatened Phoenix Rebel, so if anything happens to him, he'll know who did it. Just stay out of my life and never threaten Phoenix again." She turned toward the door, but Gunnar stood in her way.

"You're not leaving here with that high and mighty attitude. You stay away from Phoenix Rebel or I'll hurt him so bad you'll never recognize him."

"Gunnar!" Rosie was surprised when Cindy joined the conversation. "If you harm one hair on that man's head or on Rosie's, I will leave you and I will take my children and you will never see them again."

"Shut up, Cindy."

Cindy marched toward the stairs.

"Where are you going?"

She threw the dish towel on the floor. "Leaving. A family who would do what they did to Rosie is a family I do not want to be part of. This time I won't be coming back."

"Stop it!" Rosie shouted. "I don't want to come between you and Gunnar. That's your problem, and I don't want any part of it. I just want to make it very clear that my life is my own, and I will not stand for any of you to interfere with it. That's my bottom line."

Gunnar grabbed her arm and squeezed. "How dare you…"

"You should know Sheriff Carson is waiting at the road. If I don't come out of here in thirty minutes, he'll be coming in. And you'll be going to jail."

"Let her go." Malachi spoke for the first time. "This

whole family is screwed up. I almost lost my wife and kids over a Rebel fight, and I'm not going to do that again. I'm not taking part in hurting Phoenix. I'll lose my kids."

Gunnar let go of her arm and glanced at their father.

Ira McCray nodded his head. "Let her go," he muttered so low she barely heard it.

Gunnar let go and headed for the stairs. "Cindy, c'mon. I was just trying to scare her. Cindy!"

Rosie stepped closer to her father. "I will marry Phoenix Rebel."

He looked at her then, his eyes glazed over with something she couldn't define. Could it possibly be regret? "Kate Rebel will never allow her son to marry you. You're dreaming."

Turning, she swung toward the door, not letting her father's words deter her. She'd come here with a purpose and she'd accomplished it. Now she had her whole future ahead of her. Her future with Phoenix.

# Chapter Fifteen

Phoenix spent the morning in Gabe's office, talking with Levi Coyote on the phone. The PI had run a thorough background check on Valerie Green Stephens and her husband, Colonel Kyle Stephens. Levi was immediately contacted by the FBI to cease and desist his investigation of Colonel Stephens. Levi had explained that he was only interested in talking to the colonel about his wife and had nothing to do with national security or anything else. He was still waiting for the okay to do that.

The call from Colonel Stephens was crucial. He could answer a lot of questions about the future for Jake and why Valerie suddenly wanted custody of her child. It might be a pipe dream, but they all were waiting for that call.

In the meantime Levi had found out other details. Valerie was back in Colorado a month after her grandmother had passed away. She had hired a good lawyer, and it had taken weeks to get her case heard. Eventually she'd had the custody ruling overturned because the court hadn't done enough to locate her.

Valerie and her husband could offer Jake a family environment. Phoenix tried to impress upon Gabe what Jake needed was much more than that—he needed a parent who put him first. But as the hours dwindled, his chance of keeping Jake was getting smaller and smaller. But Gabe kept working, as did Levi.

IN THE LATE AFTERNOON, Gabe said he had to go home, and there was nothing else they could do until the hearing in the morning. Phoenix checked his phone a dozen times to see if Rosie had called. She hadn't. He went home, packed a bag and headed for Austin so he could be in court early. Gabe said he would be there early, too.

Phoenix checked in to a hotel and waited. He called Rosie one more time just because he had to. Where was she? He needed her tomorrow more than he'd ever needed anyone in his life.

ON THE WAY HOME, Rosie's father's words kept running through her mind: *Kate Rebel will never allow her son to marry you.* As her truck ate up the miles, her bravado died. She didn't want Phoenix to have to choose between her and his family, and that's what it would come down to. Finally she had to admit her father was right. Kate Rebel would never allow one of her sons to marry a McCray.

That's why Phoenix had never mentioned to his mother that he was seeing Rosie. Phoenix knew her reaction would not be good, and he'd put it off as long as he could. It didn't mean he didn't love her. It just meant their relationship was complicated because of their two families.

She went into her trailer and fished her phone out from the bottom of her purse. It was dead. She hadn't used it in days. She wanted to talk to Phoenix, just to hear his voice. She put her phone on to charge and went outside to feed the horses. They still were fidgety from being pinned up in the corral. She opened the gate and let them out into the pasture to romp and play to their hearts' content. She leaned on the fence, watching. Was it possible to have a future with Phoenix? They would be disowned from both sides of the families. They would be alone, just the two of them and Jake. What kind of future could they have? Tired of the questions going around in her head, she called the horses and put them back in the corral. They would go into their stalls for the night to stay out of the cold.

Rosie went inside and made a sandwich. She sat at the booth, eating and drinking orange juice because it made her feel closer to Phoenix. Afterward she took her phone off charge and sat on the sofa, holding it in her hand. She had to call to let him know she was okay. In a few minutes…

When Rosie awoke, it was five in the morning and she was still on the sofa with the phone in her hand. Dixie whined, lying next to her. She had to talk to Phoenix to sort out her feelings, and she had to do it now. Well, it might be a little early. But she would do it soon. She couldn't keep avoiding something that might hurt her more than she ever wanted to be hurt.

After a shower and breakfast, she opened the phone and saw she had thirty-two messages from Phoenix. As she read the texts, a chill settled around her heart. *No! No! They took Jake from him.* How could that happen? How could she have left her phone off all this time? He needed her and she wasn't there. She quickly scanned the address he'd given her and ran to get dressed, slipping on a long Western-style skirt and a brown turtleneck sweater. She pulled on brown leather boots, grabbed her purse, Dixie and dashed to her truck. Her hair and makeup she would do in the truck. The hearing was at ten, and she would be there to support him come hell or high water.

When she reached the address, there were a lot of trucks in the parking lot, but she found a spot. She stroked Dixie and cracked a window for her. She got out and came face-to-face with Kate Rebel. Another Rebel son stood behind her with a woman, Jenny Walker. Rosie remembered her from school.

Her nerves stretched like an electric wire, tight and hot. She was hoping Mrs. Rebel would move on, but her hope died as the woman walked up to her.

"Mom." Her son tried to stop her.

"It's okay, Quincy," Mrs. Rebel said. "I have something to say and I'm going to say it."

Rosie's backbone stiffened at the woman's tone.

"Please leave my son alone. He thinks he loves you, but he doesn't. He's just infatuated and intrigued with you. It won't last long, believe me. I know him because I'm his mother. He's fighting for his son and he doesn't need you here today."

From somewhere deep within her, Rosie found the strength to answer. "All my life I've heard only good things about you, Mrs. Rebel, but evidently the rumors were false."

"What do you mean?"

"I've heard that you love your sons and would do anything for them. That must be wrong, because a mother would want what was best for her son. But you're more interested in what's best for you, and that's not having to deal with a McCray. That's not love. That's manipulation. Most mothers love and support their children even when it hurts."

The woman's face crumpled into a deep frown. "Please just let him go and leave us in peace."

Rosie turned back to her truck. "You don't have to worry about me, Mrs. Rebel."

Inside the truck she trembled so severely she had to grip the steering wheel for support. Dixie crawled into her lap, and she held on to her for dear life. This was where she gave up and went back to her trailer and stopped believing in fairy tales. She and Phoenix didn't have a future, not with his mother standing between them. There would be no happily-ever-after for them.

She leaned her head on the steering wheel, wondering where she went from here. Everything she wanted was inside that courtroom. Could she drive away and not help Phoenix keep Jake?

PHOENIX WAS WORRIED, not knowing how this day would end. And worried that Rosie hadn't called. His whole world was crashing down around him, and he needed to be strong to face this day without her. His whole family arrived, and they even brought baby John and baby Justin. The Rebels packed the small courtroom. He was happy they were there, but there was one person missing...

He sat with Gabe at a table and stared as Valerie walked in with her lawyer—a very polished Valerie compared with the buckle bunny he remembered from the rodeo. She wore a nice dress and heels, and as he watched her, Phoenix wondered what had drawn him to her. She seemed emotionless and cold. But then, years ago he hadn't exactly been looking at other qualities, just her body. That showed his immaturity, and he hoped he had grown in the intervening years.

"Stay positive," Gabe said to him. "You're a good father, and the judge will look at that."

The bailiff introduced Judge Margaret Cobain, and she came in and took a seat. She perused a folder and an iPad on her desk. "I see I have a Colorado case dumped in my court, and I'm trying to figure out why. Baby boy Jake Rebel now resides in Texas with his father, and the judge in Colorado ordered the case to be heard here because of the boy's residency. Do you have a problem with that Mrs. Stephens?"

"No, Your Honor. I just want my son."

"That's what we're here to decide today." The judge looked at Valerie's lawyer, and the woman stood up and spoke. "Mrs. Stephens's maternal rights were terminated because no one bothered to take the time to locate her. She is the mother and she has a right to raise her child. Circumstances prevented her from doing that after the boy was born. Mrs. Stephens's husband is a colonel in army intelligence. His job sends him all over the world, and Mrs. Stephens wasn't able to take Jake with her at that time. Her grandmother agreed to keep the baby. But now she's ready for them to be a family."

"Why did you not leave a forwarding address with your grandmother?" the judge asked Valerie.

"It was there in her house. I don't know why no one found it. I called her weekly to check on my baby. You have the phone records. I never abandoned my child."

"I see." The judge flipped through some papers.

Valerie's lawyer continued, "Mrs. Stephens appreciates Mr. Rebel stepping forward and taking care of her son when she couldn't, but the baby belongs with his mother, and we hope the court will grant Mrs. Stephens full custody."

The judge looked at Gabe and he stood and explained what had happened since Phoenix had found out he was Jake's father. "Mr. Rebel is a loving, caring father, and he has bonded with Jake. He has taken full responsibility, and I see no reason to take the child from him now. Mrs. Stephens had ample opportunity to be a mother, but she didn't exercise that right. I fully believe Mr. Rebel is the right parent for Jake, and it would be devastating to the child to remove him from his father now."

"Mr. Rebel, your job concerns me. How do you plan to take care of Jake while you're riding the rodeo circuit? A child should have a home, a family environment."

Phoenix stood. "I realize that, and if I have to, I can quit the circuit and raise my son. For now, I take him with me everywhere I go. Also, my girlfriend helps me. We have a live-in horse trailer, and Jake is in bed by nine o'clock, but he won't go to sleep until I'm there."

"So you're in a relationship with someone?"

"Yes, Your Honor, and I plan to marry her."

His mother gasped behind him, but Phoenix ignored her.

"Why isn't she here today?"

Phoenix clenched his fists. "She will be. She's just running late." He prayed with all his might he was right.

"It's very admirable that you're willing to give up your career."

"I'll do anything to keep my son."

"This is a very difficult decision. I firmly believe a mother has a right to raise her child. In these early years, especially, a child needs his mother."

"No offense, Your Honor, but a child needs his father, too."

"I don't dis—" The judge looked to the back of the room.

Ms. Connors stood in the doorway, looking harassed. Her blouse was out of her slacks and her hair was mussed. "I'm sorry, Your Honor. I'm Ms. Connors from CPS. We have a problem with Jake Rebel."

"What kind of problem?" the judge asked with a lifted eyebrow.

"He somehow got out of the room we were in, and now…we can't find him."

"He's two years old, Ms. Connors. He has to be here somewhere."

Phoenix fumed. "Your Honor, he did that when his great-grandmother passed away. He was looking for her and now he's looking for me. What have they done with my kid?"

"I'm wondering the same thing, Mr. Rebel." The judge looked squarely at Ms. Connors.

"Ms. Henshaw is looking and I'll go help her," Ms. Connors said, quickly leaving.

Phoenix had had enough. He'd started around the desk when he saw Jake crawled through the doorway in nothing but a diaper. He crawled beneath the chairs and straight to Phoenix. He pulled up on Phoenix's jeans, and Phoenix lifted his son into his arms.

"Daddy gone. Daddy gone." Jake wailed into his shoulder with loud sobs.

Phoenix patted his back. "No. Daddy's here. See, Daddy's here." He kissed his son's cheek and Jake clutched him tight around the neck, refusing to raise his head.

Ms. Connors appeared in the doorway. "Oh, thank goodness. He's here."

"Yes," the judge replied. "I'm wondering how CPS can be so inept as to lose track of one little boy."

"The boy has resisted ever since we took him. Children usually settle down, but not this one. He wouldn't eat or drink his milk, and he would get out the door, and the foster parents would have to search for him. They dress him, but he takes off his clothes immediately. Jake Rebel has been a big problem. We'll be happy to turn him over to one of his parents today."

Phoenix tossed his keys to Paxton. "His diaper bag is in my truck."

Jake continued to cry on Phoenix's shoulder, and Phoenix continued to console him. As each minute passed, anger filled Phoenix at what had been done to his child.

Paxton came back, and Phoenix laid Jake on the table to change his diaper because he was wet. He didn't care if the judge liked it or not. The judge didn't say a word as he changed the diaper, sat in a chair and pulled on Jake's jeans and boots.

"Mine. Boots." Jake pointed, his face red from crying.

"Yes. Those are your boots and your jeans." Phoenix then slipped a Western shirt on Jake and tucked it into his jeans. He added the belt with the buckle.

"Mine," Jake said.

"Yes, that's your belt buckle, just like Daddy's."

Phoenix stood with his son in his arms, and Jake did something Phoenix really wished he hadn't. "Beer, Daddy."

The room became so quiet the traffic could be heard from outside. Phoenix looked at Ms. Connors. "Do you have some milk?"

The woman immediately brought him a container of

milk, and Phoenix poured it into a SpongeBob sippy cup. As Jake sipped hungrily on it, Phoenix walked closer to the judge.

"Tell the judge what this is?" Phoenix tapped the sippy cup.

Jake stared at the judge with big rounded eyes.

"Tell her."

"Beer," Jake said loudly. Then Phoenix told the judge how Jake came to call milk beer. "It was the only way to get him off the bottle. At the foster home I took him from, the lady told me it was time for him to be off the bottle, and I did what I had to."

"You can sit down, Mr. Rebel." The judge glanced through more papers on her desk. "Mrs. Stephens, I see your visits with Jake didn't go very well."

Valerie stood. "No, but I feel that will change once he gets to know me. I am his mother, and I love him and want him in my life. I will do everything I can to make that happen."

Phoenix could tell the judge was leaning toward Valerie and there was nothing he could do. Rosie's absence today meant he'd lost her. He couldn't lose Jake, too. His world was crumbling around him and he was powerless to stop it. A Rebel was supposed to be strong, but his strength was waning. He had his family, but today it wasn't enough.

Jake sat on Phoenix's lap, all happy now, no tears in sight. Phoenix hoped the judge saw that and understood he and Jake had a bond. A father-and-son bond that shouldn't be broken.

"Momma, Daddy." Jake looked up at him, and Phoenix didn't know how to explain to his son that Rosie wasn't here.

"Son…" Words clogged his throat.

"Momma." Jake pointed to the back of the room, and Phoenix stared at the woman standing there. *Rosie.* She'd come. His heart lifted in a way he couldn't explain. It had been on life support and now it was beating crazily for her.

Jake scurried off his lap and ran to Rosie. She picked him up and kissed his cheek, smiling. It was clear to see how much they loved each other, and Phoenix hoped the judge was looking.

"Ma'am, what are you doing in my courtroom?" the judge asked.

"I'm Rosemary Wilcott, and I'm here to support Phoenix and Jake." Rosie walked to Phoenix's side, holding Jake. He slipped his left arm around her waist and pulled her close.

"I've never been so glad to see anyone in my whole life," he whispered for her ears only.

"I'm sorry I turned off my phone," she whispered back.

He looked into her beautiful blue eyes. "Did you change your mind?"

She nodded. "Several times."

"I'm just happy you're here. The judge is about to rule on who gets custody."

Before the judge could speak, a tall man with broad shoulders walked in. He wore jeans, a white shirt and a cowboy hat. He shook hands with Gabe and handed him some papers. "You owe me a drink." Phoenix knew it had to be Levi Coyote.

"You got it," Gabe said, reading through the papers.

Levi shook Phoenix's hand and walked toward the door.

"Mr. Coyote, it's not often we see you in Family Court."

He winked at the judge. "I'm everywhere."

"I'm guessing those papers have something to do with this case, Mr. Garrison."

Gabe stood and took the papers to her. "Yes, Your Honor."

"Well, I had already made my decision, but this puts a whole new light on the case." She looked at Valerie. "Mrs. Stephens, it seems your husband is looking for you. You left your villa in Italy without a word as to your whereabouts. Seems you're good at doing that."

"That's invading my privacy. How dare they investigate me!"

"Your husband states that the calls to your grandmother were about money and not about the boy."

"He's lying."

"Do you really want to go there, Mrs. Stephens? He has cut off your credit card because of excessive spending and has put you on an allowance. He also states he has an ex and three grown children. He's not interested in raising another child."

"He doesn't mean that."

"I'm inclined to believe a colonel in army intelligence."

"This doesn't concern him. I am my grandmother's only heir, and I have a right to her estate."

"Excuse me?" the judge said in disbelief.

"This has been about money?" Phoenix could no longer stay quiet. "You think your grandmother had money and you want it?"

"It belongs to me!" Valerie shouted.

"Your grandmother had a small savings account," the judge informed her, "and she left that for Jake's education. There was nothing else."

"That's not true. My grandmother pinched pennies, and I know she had money. She just never would give it to me."

"You can have the money, Valerie," Phoenix broke in. "Just leave Jake with me."

"Hold on, cowboy. I make the decisions in this courtroom," the judge interrupted. "The money stays with the boy. I had already made this decision, but now I'll make it legal. I grant full and permanent custody of Jake Rebel to his father, Phoenix Rebel. Any visitation will be at Mr. Rebel's discretion. And you, Mrs. Stephens, will be lucky if I don't file charges against you for using this court's time for needless greed. This court is adjourned. Good luck, Mr. Rebel."

Valerie walked out with her lawyer following her. Phoenix supposed she didn't want any visitation rights, not that he was inclined to grant her any. He hoped that would be the last he would ever see of her.

The Rebel family clapped, and Phoenix embraced Rosie and Jake. He had the whole world in his arms and it was all he needed. These two people in his life. Forever.

"I love you, Rosie," he whispered. "I said I wouldn't pressure you, but will you marry me? In this courthouse today?"

"Oh, Phoenix."

"Just say yes."

"Yes."

He turned to face his family. "I'm going to marry Rosemary McCray Wilcott here today, and we would love your presence. If you don't come, that's okay. I just want you to know you're invited."

"Phoenix, don't do this," his mother implored. "You've only just met this woman."

"Her name is Rosie."

"I'm not giving advice, Phoenix, but what's the rush? Give us time to get to know her and we'll have a big wedding at the ranch." Quincy was doing his usual thing, trying to keep the peace.

Elias got to his feet. "I say do what you want. It's your life."

His mother turned to his brother. "Be quiet, Elias."

"Everybody calm down," Falcon said.

Grandpa spoke up. "Kate, it's no secret I didn't like you when John brought you out to the ranch." Everyone took a deep breath because they knew what was coming. "I told him you're a city girl and wouldn't make him a good wife. You couldn't even cook and didn't know how to do much of anything. But he looked me right in the eye and said he loved you, and I knew he meant it. I loved my son and didn't want to lose him, so Martha and I accepted you into the family. I think it's time you sucked it up and did the same thing."

"Stay out of this, Abe."

Grandpa got to his feet, a stubborn expression etched across his face. "I will not stay out of it, missy. John was my son. His boys are all I have left of him, and I will support them to hell and back."

"Have you forgotten the McCrays killed him? I will not welcome a McCray into this family."

"The McCrays didn't kill him. Booze did, and you never lifted a finger to stop it. That's on you, missy."

"How dare you!"

"Please stop this." Rosie's eyes glazed over with tears as she stared at Phoenix. "I can't do this. I can't come between you and your family. We would never be happy."

"Rosie." He pulled her to his side. "We can do this. We can make it work."

She shook her head. "The feud will always come between us, and we can't build our lives on so much turmoil. Our love is tearing your family apart, and it's tearing me apart." She kissed Jake's cheek and handed him to Phoenix. "Take care of Jake. I love you…but please don't call or text me. It's over and we have to let go. Please…"

She ran from the room, and Phoenix made no move to stop her. He knew from the sadness in her eyes it was over. But letting go wasn't in his nature. He would never love anyone the way he loved Rosie.

"It's for the best, son."

He looked at his mother, trying not to let his anger get the best of him. "It's not what's best for me. I'm going back to the bunkhouse and pack my things and then Jake and I are leaving for Vegas."

"What about Thanksgiving?"

"I won't be home for Thanksgiving, and after Jake and I return from Vegas, I'll find a place to live, because I'll never return to Rebel Ranch."

"No! You can't do that. What about your legacy? Your father wanted you to have part of the ranch. You know that. You just need some time to come to grips with this."

"I don't need time, Mom. Dad always told me to lead with my heart when I had a problem, and that's what I'm doing. If he were here, I know he would accept Rosie, because that's the only way to peel away the layers of bitterness and hatred so the healing can begin from the tragedy that has affected many people. That's what my father would've wanted, and I feel no guilt in walking away, because I take a part of him where ever I go." He picked up the diaper bag and walked out of the courtroom with Jake in his arms, feeling stronger than he had in a long time.

"Quincy, do something. Talk to him."

"No, Mom. I'm not talking to Phoenix. He's made up his mind. I have to respect that and so do you."

"Quincy!"

# Chapter Sixteen

Rosie drove away with tears in her eyes, but she knew she was doing the right thing. She couldn't break up the Rebel family. It would just be one more thing fueling the feud. They couldn't build a happy life on heartache and pain. As much is it hurt, she kept driving.

Dixie barked from her bed in the backseat.

"It's okay, Dixie. We're going home."

Home wouldn't be home anymore without Phoenix and Jake. There were just too many wonderful memories. Good thing she would be moving soon. After the National Finals Rodeo, she would start looking for a new place to stable her horses and park her trailer. She would start over once again.

But this time the heartache would linger for a long, long time.

The tears were blinding her, so she pulled over at a convenience store. She wiped tears away with the back of her hand and took a deep breath. Their love wasn't meant to be.

WHEN PHOENIX MADE it back to the bunkhouse, Jake screeched with delight, running around, grabbing his things and saying, "Mine. Mine. Mine."

His son had missed being home and now Phoenix would uproot him once again, but he would be there to help him make the adjustment. It had to be done and he didn't see any other way. He was just glad to have his son back, and he was going to make sure Jake had a happy future.

While Jake played, Phoenix packed a bag for both of them. He got a flight out early in the morning, and he wanted to get Jake in bed as soon as possible so he would be rested. He tried not to think about Rosie because it would hurt too much. But tonight he knew he would feel the pain of losing her. He had to prove to her she meant more to him than his family, the rodeo or anything. She and Jake were his life.

A knock sounded at the door, and Phoenix groaned. He didn't want to have to deal with his family again. Elias stood there. His brother was his own man and he did his own thing. At times Elias came across as unemotional and uncaring, but he'd stood up for Phoenix today, and Phoenix would remember that. Maybe there was more to his brother than he'd ever dreamed.

"Hey," Phoenix said, opening the door. "I'm not really in the mood to talk to anyone."

"I just wanted to see if you needed anything...like money."

"No, thanks."

"Stand up for what you want. That's what Dad always told us. I'm proud you're taking a stand because I can see how much you love her. Good luck, man." He patted Phoenix's shoulder and walked out.

Phoenix never thought the brother he fought with the most would be the one who would stand beside him. Before he could move away from the door, he saw Quincy and Falcon coming his way. He groaned inwardly. Was he going to have to deal with all of them?

He held the door open. "I really have nothing else to say, and if you're here to change my mind, you're wasting your time."

"We just wanted to make sure you're okay."

"No, I'm not okay." He didn't lie. "But I will be."

"If you need anything, you know how to contact us," Quincy said. "Anything."

"Thanks, but I have to do this on my own. My way."

Quincy hugged him, as did Falcon, and they walked out the door.

In that moment, Phoenix realized his brothers finally understood he'd grown up, and they were accepting his decision because they considered him adult enough to make it. That was awesome and gave him the strength he needed to keep forging ahead.

Egan, Jude, Rico and Paxton came in later and also offered their support. Phoenix thanked them and that was it. No one pressured him to make amends with his mother. His mother had her own way of thinking and he accepted that. It just wasn't his way. It would be hard to walk away from Rebel Ranch, but he was prepared to risk it all for love.

That night after supper, Paxton nagged him about the rodeo and Vegas. "How are you going to handle Jake at the rodeo?"

"I'll improvise and I'm sure a few cowboys will help me, including you."

"You bet. But it was much easier when Rosie was around."

Phoenix pushed the food around on his plate, letting

the image of Rosie slip through his defenses. He had to stop or he wouldn't be able to do what he had to.

"I'll go with you and take care of Jake," Rico said.

Phoenix eyed his friend. "You never leave Horseshoe."

"I've never seen you and Paxton ride except on television. I think I might like to experience that in person."

"Really?"

"Sure. I'll talk to Falcon and your mom in the morning, but I don't see a problem."

"Mom may disagree."

"I don't think your mom will keep me from taking care of Jake, especially since Rosie's out of the picture."

"Rico, thanks, but..."

"No buts."

"Come on, Phoenix," Paxton said. "We need someone to entertain Jake, and Jake likes Rico. Accept this gift and stop being so pigheaded."

And it was settled. Rico would come to Vegas and take care of Jake while Phoenix rode.

Early the next morning, Phoenix drove away from Rebel Ranch. Since Paxton and Rico were staying for Thanksgiving, they would fly out later.

Phoenix would spend Thanksgiving in Vegas with his son. Alone. Without Rosie.

ROSIE WAS BUSY getting ready for the long drive to Vegas. She planned to leave before Thanksgiving so Lady would have time to get acclimated.

The pain inside her was strong and she tried to ignore it. She was hoping it would fade, but her heart ached and all she wanted to do was cry. She would get better. It would take time.

If only she could stop thinking about him... They'd

talked about making the trip together with Jake. Now, once again, she would be alone. For a brief moment in time she'd known what it was like to be happy, and she treasured that.

The Tisdales would feed her horses while she was away. Everything packed, she was ready to pull out. On impulse she called Haley. She didn't have to be lonely. That had always been her choice, but not anymore.

"Hey, when are you leaving?" Rosie asked.

"This morning."

"Would you like some company? Since we both live in Texas, I figured we could do this together and make the trip less lonely. Unless you have other plans."

"What about Phoenix?"

"I'll explain later."

"Sounds great."

"Where do you want to meet?"

"I live outside Lampasas, and you can just stop by on your way." Haley gave the address and Rosie wrote it down.

That settled, Rosie felt a little better. When Rosie reached Sonora, she and Haley decided to go in Rosie's trailer with the horses. They talked along the way, and Rosie opened her heart and shared what had happened with Phoenix.

"I'm sorry."

"It's going to be hard to see him at the rodeo."

"Just hang in there. He loves you and you love him. I wouldn't give up just yet."

"You haven't met his mother."

Haley laughed, and Rosie found herself laughing too. Maybe there was hope for her. Maybe she could move on without Phoenix. The next couple of weeks would tell the tale.

VEGAS WAS LIKE no place on earth. The lights were blinding, the noise deafening, and the excitement and energy stirred Phoenix's blood to fever pitch. He and Jake had made it to the National Finals Rodeo. The fact that this was his last ride kept running through his head, but he didn't feel bad about it. He was ready to move on with his life. He would give this last rodeo all he had and more.

He checked in to the MGM Grand Hotel. He'd asked for a baby bed for Jake and was glad to see it in the room. The suite had two bedrooms and a small living area. Paxton and Rico would share the other bedroom. It had twin beds.

He rented a car with a car seat, and he and Jake set out to explore Vegas and to see the sights. They toured an aquarium, a theme park and the Hoover Dam, but Jake enjoyed a regular park best, where he could run and play. They had Thanksgiving at a quaint little diner, and he never missed Rosie more than he did sitting there without her, wondering where she was. They'd planned to drive out together, and he worried about her driving by herself. She was very efficient and responsible. She would be okay, but that didn't ease the ache in his chest.

Paxton and Rico arrived the day after Thanksgiving and things got hectic in the room. Jake was so excited to see them, running around, showing them where they would sleep and where he would sleep. Jake had a family and he knew who they were.

"I've got some news for you," Paxton said. "The whole family's coming out for the rodeo except for Jude's and Egan's families. They will fly out next Friday for the last two nights."

"Who will be watching the ranch?" Phoenix was puzzled by this. If this was his mother's way of trying to support him and convince him to come back home, it wasn't going to work.

"Wyatt's deputies are going to patrol our road and keep an eye out. The McCrays have been very quiet lately and we don't expect any trouble."

That would be the best gift: if the Rebels and Mc-Crays could live peacefully together. He was dreaming, but then, he'd always been a dreamer.

And so it began. A week of grueling competition. The best cowboys and cowgirls were in Vegas to compete for gold buckles and money.

The National Finals Rodeo started with a bang in the opening ceremony. All the cowboys and cowgirls rode into the arena to meet the crowd. Phoenix and Paxton rode together and waved to the family sitting in the stands. Jake sat on Rico's lap and he waved vigorously.

Phoenix caught a glimpse of Rosie. She'd made it. That was all he needed to know.

TEN NIGHTS OF grueling competition. Rosie was doing well barrel racing. She was neck and neck with Tawny Maye from Canada for the top spot. Phoenix watched her every night and admired her grace and talent.

Bull riding was the toughest sport, but Phoenix and Paxton stayed in the top five all week. It was exhausting, but they kept competing.

When Phoenix wasn't attending sponsor meetings or doing rodeo stuff behind the scenes, he spent time with Jake. The family took in Cowboy Christmas and the Cowboy Gift Show. Phoenix didn't speak with anyone, but he heard it all from Pax. His mom and sisters-in-law enjoyed the shows at the convention center. The family always had dinner together, but Phoenix returned to the room with Jake. He wasn't being difficult. He was sticking to his principles.

Jake did very well with Rico. Phoenix explained that Jake had to sit with Rico while he worked, and as long as Jake could see him, he was okay.

It all came down to the last night. So far Phoenix and Paxton had made some money, as had Rosie, and now they were going for the title and the championship in their events.

It was the last night and Rosie had a slight lead over Tawny. Tonight would decide the winner.

In Lady's pen, Rosie tried to calm the horse. She was always nervous and fidgety before a race, but tonight she seemed to be more antsy than ever. Rosie stroked her face and rubbed her neck.

"Calm down, girl. We can do this."

Lady threw up her head and snorted, and Rosie kept stroking her.

"Hey."

Rosie looked up to see Haley leaning on the fence.

"I just came over to wish you luck. I'll be rooting for you, but with all the Rebels here, I don't think you need my support."

"I'm not sure if they're rooting for me."

"Looks like it to me. Phoenix watches you every night."

She'd noticed, but it didn't change anything. They weren't meant for each other.

"Do you want to leave in the morning?"

"Yeah. Probably early. We'll talk later."

"You bet. Ride like the wind."

Someone called to them. "Time to line up." She swung

into the saddle, talking soothingly to Lady. Trotting the horse out of the pen, Lady danced around, ready to run. She hated the waiting.

Haley was ten horses ahead of Rosie, and her score wasn't good. Rosie knew she was disappointed. She could hear the announcer and knew it was getting close to her time.

Tawny was ahead of her and Rosie listened, hoping to hear her score. Fourteen point one. That would be hard to beat. She had to race her best and that's what she was prepared to do. Lady danced sideways down the chute. Rosie was trying to control her. Times like this, though, the horse had a lot of energy.

"You're up," the handler shouted, walking beside her. *Stay calm.*

She gave the thumbs-up sign and danced Lady down the long chute leading into the arena.

The announcer's voice came on: "Next up we have a little lady from Temple, Texas, Rosemary Wilcott. Let's see what she can do on her horse named Golden Lady."

Taking a deep breath, she dug her heels in, and with Lady's high energy she catapulted them into the arena. At this point Rosie blocked out everything. The noise, the crowd and everything else in her head. It was just barrel racing.

She started the clover-leaf pattern on the right, always. Lady dashed around the barrel with ease, kicking up dirt as they made the turn for the barrel on the left. Once around the left barrel, Lady charged for the last barrel. They made the circle around the third barrel and Rosie leaned forward in the saddle, urging Lady on, full speed ahead.

"Go, go, go," she repeated over and over as Lady

charged back into the chute at breakneck speed. Fourteen point zero. She heard the score and raised her fist. "We did it. We did it!" She'd won the title. She could barely breathe as people congratulated her. And then she raced Lady out for her victory lap, waving to the crowd.

Dismounting, gulping for air, she saw a cowboy running toward her in full bull-riding gear, spurs, chaps, protective vest and a black shirt with his sponsors' names on his sleeves.

*Phoenix.*

What was he doing here? Bull riding was next. Then she knew, and she started running toward him. This was what love was about: needing each other.

He grabbed her and swung her around and around. "Congratulations! I know you said not to call or… I had to see you."

She touched a finger to his lips. "Shh." And then she wrapped her arms around his neck and held him, loving the scent of leather, dirt and horses that lingered in the air and mingled with the touch of him.

Everything was perfect when it was just the two of them.

But it wasn't just the two them. Two feuding families stood between them.

He kissed the tip of her nose. "Gotta go."

As he ran toward the chutes, his spurs jangling, she whispered, "I love you."

But was love enough?

# Chapter Seventeen

Phoenix hurried back to bull riding. Paxton met him.

"Where have you been? I've been looking all over for you. Bull riding has already started."

"I had to see Rosie."

Paxton shook his head. "Man, you got it bad. So, are you getting back together?"

"I don't know."

They walked toward the cowboy deck. "Could I talk to you about something?"

"Sure."

"Lisa's been texting me."

Phoenix sighed. "Are you talking to her?" Lisa was Pax's ex-fiancée. Last year she'd ruined the finals for Pax with her temperamental ways.

"No. I'm just…"

Phoenix slapped him on the back. "Focus on bull riding and forget about Lisa. The Rebel boys have to finish one and two. I don't care who's one. I just care that one of us wins this thing."

They high-fived. "You got it."

Phoenix stood on the cowboy's deck and watched the first twelve cowboys ride. The highest score had been eighty-eight. It all came down to the last three riders,

Dakota Janaway, Paxton and Phoenix. Dakota was up next on a bull called Fool's Gold. The bull bucked and twisted but Dakota stayed on and scored eighty-nine. It was up to Paxton and Phoenix to beat that or settle for second and third place.

Phoenix looked up and saw Rosie on the big-screen TV, talking to a reporter. As he watched her smiling face, he knew the biggest prize was yet to come: winning Rosie's heart.

Paxton was up next. Phoenix helped him with his bull rope, and then he slapped him on the shoulder. "Good luck, brother. We worked all year for this. Do your best."

Paxton nodded his head, completely in the mode of riding, shutting out everything else. He'd drawn a bull called Widow Maker.

Paxton raised his hand and the bull leaped from the chute with jumps, bucks and turns. Paxton rode his best and when the eight-second buzzer went off, he jumped from the bull and stood with both arms in the air. The ride was good and everyone kept their eyes on the scoreboard. When the score came up, the Rebel family stood and cheered. Ninety was the highest score of the night.

Phoenix could see Jake on Rico's shoulders, clapping. His boy was waiting for his dad. Phoenix climbed the chute, sliding onto a bull named Pearly Gates, one of the meanest bulls on the circuit and bucking bull of the year. He was known for twisting until he dislodged the cowboy. Phoenix had ridden him only twice before, and both times he'd been bucked off. But tonight he would give it his all.

The announcer's voice echoed over Phoenix's head: "Next up we have the younger Rebel brother, Phoenix. He's got his work cut out for him to beat his brother Paxton. These brothers hail from Horseshoe, Texas, and all the Rebel family is here to cheer them on. He won the title last year. Let's see what he can do on Pearly Gates, a bull known for his mean disposition."

Phoenix worked the bull rope with his gloved hand until he had it just right between his fingers. The bull stank and had a bad case of diarrhea that clogged Phoenix's senses. Good thing he'd learned to control his weak stomach or he'd be barfing right about now. Thank you, Jake.

*This is for you, Dad.*

*And Rosie.*

As he raised his left hand, the gate swung open and Pearly Gates jumped into the arena with fire-and-brimstone momentum. He bucked and kicked out with his back legs and then went into a spin. Phoenix held on, trying to maintain his posture and rhythm and to spur when he needed to. Just when he thought he had it, the bull turned and spun in the other direction. Phoenix grew dizzy and wondered just how long eight seconds was. He surely had been on the bull for over a minute.

The buzzer sounded like a bomb. Phoenix leaped from the bull, but the bull turned and caught Phoenix with his head, catapulting him into the dirt. The bullfighters kept the bull away and rushed him back into the chute. The dizziness intensified and Phoenix lay for moment, unable to move. A hush came over the crowd. He faded in and out of consciousness. The first face he saw was his Dad's. The last was Rosie's.

"Phoenix!"

He blinked and saw Paxton's worried face. Several other rodeo people gathered round. He had to get up.

"Are you okay?" Paxton asked.

"Yeah." Phoenix managed to stand. A roar erupted from the crowd. Bordered by Paxton and their friend Cole, he walked out of the arena and waited for the score.

"Phoenix!" He turned to see Rosie running toward him. "Are you okay?"

He caught her. "I'm better now."

She wrapped her arms around him and he held on as they waited for the score. When ninety-one popped up, he squeezed her so tight she laughed.

"Ladies and gentlemen, Phoenix Rebel has repeated as bull-riding champion. Congratulations! I believe that's Rosemary Wilcott, the barrel-racing champion, down there with him. Do we have a behind-the-scenes romance going on? Come on out and y'all take a bow for the crowd."

"Ready?" He smiled into her eyes.

She took his hand, and they walked out into the arena to the roar of the crowd. Suddenly Jake was there. Rico had brought him down. Phoenix held him, and Jake waved along with them.

"A new generation of Rebels. Congratulations to the Rebel family."

The last ride was the easiest of all because it came with the biggest prize: Rosie and Jake.

Now he had to make it happen.

WHEN THEY WALKED out of the arena, his whole family was waiting for them. His mother hugged him.

"I'm so glad you're okay."

"I'm fine, Mom."

He turned to his family. "While I was here before Thanksgiving, I found a little church about five blocks away. Not a sleazy one on the strip. It's small. Country-looking." He gave the address. "You can't miss it. I'm going to marry Rosemary McCray Wilcott there just as soon as we finish here, and we would love your presence."

"Phoenix—" Rosie began.

He put a finger over her lips. "We love each other and we should be together. Please meet me there after the awards ceremony. I talked to the minister and he will wait for us."

"We can do it later."

"No. If you love me, you'll be there." He knew he was being pushy, but he was fighting for their love.

"Phoenix..." She wrapped her arms around him and Jake, and Phoenix felt her love all the way to his soul. But he felt something else, too. She was pulling away. Those damn doubts.

She rested her face against his for a moment and then walked into the crowd.

"Momma," Jake called, but Rosie didn't stop.

Phoenix looked at his family. "I'm going to that church to wait for Rosie. I'll wait there forever if I have to. That's how much I love her. If you want to join me, you're welcome. Jake and I know what we want."

He handed Jake to Rico. "I have to get my stuff out of the locker room and then I have the awards ceremony. I'll meet you back at the hotel."

"Sure thing."

"Son, it's clear this girl doesn't want to marry you," his mom said. "Please, let's go to the hotel and have a nice meal to celebrate."

His mother kept beating that same old drum. So he did the only thing he could. He hugged her. "I'm sorry this is so difficult for you. The last thing I wanted was to hurt you. I'm asking you again to give Rosie a chance."

He kissed her cheek and strolled away with a heavy heart, but his spirits were high because he believed in his and Rosie's love.

ROSIE WAS ALL nerves and couldn't seem to keep her thoughts straight. Phoenix wanted to get married. Tonight. In Vegas. With his whole family present. But his mother still hated her.

"Rosie?"

She became aware someone was calling her name and turned to Haley.

"What?"

"You were in another time zone."

"Phoenix wants to get married. Right now." She blurted out the words, unable to keep them inside. She had to talk to someone.

Haley lifted an eyebrow. "Is that a problem?"

"His mother. I don't want to cause a rift between him and his mother."

"So you'll give up Phoenix to please his mother."

Rosie considered that for a moment. Would she give up Phoenix to please his mother?

"No." She wasn't willing to do that.

"Well, I think you have your answer."

"It's not that simple. Phoenix loves his family and I don't want to be the one to take him away from them."

"Oh, Rosie. It is simple. Forget family. You either love Phoenix or you don't."

"Haley, it's—"

"—life," Haley finished for her. "And you have to grab it with both hands while you can."

Rosie hesitated. So much turmoil waited, yet so much love waited for her, too.

She had to make a choice.

PHOENIX HAD TRIED to catch Rosie at the awards ceremony, but she'd left quickly. He hurried back to the hotel. Jake was running around the room in his diaper, wide awake.

"He slept during the rodeo," Rico explained.

"He's up for the night."

"Yeah."

"I'll take a quick shower and then we're headed for the church."

Afterward he texted Rosie:

Jake and I are going to the church. We're staying there until you come. Love, Phoenix and Jake

Before Thanksgiving, while killing time in Vegas, Phoenix had bought them black jackets just in case. It was the only way to stay positive. He dressed Jake in a white shirt because Phoenix had a white one on. Then he put star bolo ties on both of them. Placing his Stetson on his head, he walked out of the room, holding Jake's hand.

"Pax and I will catch up with you," Rico called.

Phoenix hailed a cab. It was almost midnight. The stars were almost as bright as the lights back on the Strip. The church had a scent of candles and old wood that was inviting. He sat on the front row with Jake on his lap. The plaque outside said the church had been built in 1905. The oak pews had stood the test of time.

Jake pointed to the cross that hung above the altar. "Jesus," he said. "Ma Ma."

It had been a long time since Jake had mentioned his great-grandmother, and Phoenix wondered what was going on in his little brain. He was amazed that Jake remembered their talk about heaven. He held him a bit tighter against him.

The minister came from the altar area and walked toward them. "Mr. Rebel, I was wondering if you'd changed your mind."

"No, we're waiting for the bride, and it might be a while."

"That's okay. This is Vegas, I'm used to late night weddings." He handed him a card. "I live next door. Just call my cell when you're ready."

"Thank you."

Phoenix sat there, his heart heavy. He loved Rosie, and she had to understand that with love they could overcome all obstacles. He firmly believed that, so he was settling in for a long, long night.

Jake grew bored and scooted down to dig in the diaper bag. He found his horses and held one up. "Horse."

Phoenix let him play with the horse on the floor, just to keep him occupied. As he watched Jake on his knees, he was grateful once again that he had full custody. He wouldn't have to fight that battle again. The biggest battle was yet to be won.

The church door opened and he turned to see Paxton, Rico, Elias and Grandpa walk in. They sat in the pew behind him, and Grandpa patted his back.

"How you doing, son?"

"I don't know, Grandpa. I feel kind of dumb right now."

"She'll come." Grandpa scooted back in the pew and looked around at the church. "Did I ever tell you boys about that day I married your grandma? It was in a church just like this. She and her sister worked weeks on her wedding dress. My truck broke down and I was late getting to the church. She glared at me all through the service, and my goal was to make her smile by the end of that night. I sure made her smile."

"I thought Grandma bought her dress from a J.C. Penney catalog," Paxton said.

"Who's telling this story? That was for our twenty-fifth wedding anniversary."

"I get confused, Grandpa, with all your stories."

"If you paid attention, you wouldn't."

The door opened again. Falcon, Leah, Eden and baby John, Egan and Rachel with sleeping baby Justin, and Jude, Paige and Zane came in. They took the pews across from Phoenix. He stared at the door, hoping his mother would come. It was a long shot, but he kept hoping.

As if reading his mind, Falcon said, "Quincy's talking to her. Keep your fingers crossed."

He glanced at his brothers. "Thanks for being here."

They settled in to wait. Jake and John played with the horses on the floor and Phoenix kept glancing at his watch. The door opened again and he turned to look, hoping with all his heart it was Rosie. It wasn't. It was Quincy, Jenny and his mother. They sat next to Phoenix, his mother beside him.

"Quincy said if I didn't come, I would regret it and I...I want to be here for you, but I have so many mixed feelings."

"It's okay, Mom. It's enough that you're here. All I ask is that you give Rosie a chance. Give us a chance."

The minutes slowly ticked by. Paxton, Elias and Grandpa went outside to stretch their legs, as everyone else did at one time or another. But Phoenix kept sitting, waiting.

After two hours, Egan said they were taking the baby

back to the hotel. The family trailed out one by one, but Paxton lingered.

"C'mon on, man, face it. She's not coming."

"Go back to the hotel. I'll deal with this myself."

"I know it hurts…"

"She'll come."

Paxton threw up his hands and sat by Phoenix. "Elias and Rico are taking Grandpa to the hotel, but I'm staying. I hope they don't mind if I sleep on these pews."

Jake crawled onto Phoenix's lap, and he held his son a little tighter than he usually did. He had to hold on to something to stay positive. But as long as he believed, he would be fine.

He just had to keep believing.

ROSIE SAT IN her trailer, in turmoil as she reread Phoenix's text. He was waiting. With Jake. Doubts warred with the love inside her. All she ever wanted was to fall deeply in love and have a home and a family. She could have that with Phoenix. She could have it all, but could they be happy? Would the animosity between their two families eventually destroy their love?

She stood and screamed, the frustrated sound echoing in the trailer. She hated she had doubts. She hated her doubts were keeping them apart. She… Her eye caught something beneath the sofa. She bent down and fished it out. It was one of Jake's toy horses.

Clutching it to her chest she sank into the cushions, remembering that early morning when she had unexpectedly run into Phoenix. With his trigger-finger smile and confidence, he'd charmed his way into her heart.

She ran a finger over the horse and remembered Phoenix's confidence that Jake would love horses. He'd been right. Jake loved horses, and he loved his daddy. Suddenly staring down at the horse she knew, beyond any doubt, she loved both of them.

It didn't matter if Mrs. Rebel hated Rosie or that Rosie's father had threatened Phoenix. It only mattered that they loved each other. That love made them strong enough to face whatever obstacles they had to. It was simple, just as Haley had said.

Rosie jumped to her feet and almost stepped on Dixie. "Sorry..." A knock at the door interrupted her.

"Open up, Rosie. It's Haley."

Haley had a key. Why was she...?

"Open the door."

"Okay." As she swung the door wide, she saw Haley holding something white draped over her arms.

"Look at this." Haley marched in, bubbling with excitement as she held up a dress. It was white lace with feathers around the strapless top and the edge of the skirt, which came to mid-calf and was long in the back. It was beautiful, except for the white feathers. "It's a perfect wedding dress." Haley hiccupped on the last word.

"Have you been drinking?"

"I had a couple of beers with Cole. Just concentrate on the dress."

"Where did you get it?"

"Cole and I met this dancer at the bar in the hotel, and to make a long story short, Cole charmed her right out of her dress."

"Haley..."

"Focus on the dress, Rosie."

"It has feathers," she pointed out.

"But it's white lace and beautiful."

"Did y'all buy it?"

Haley threw an arm around Rosie's shoulders. "Here's the deal. You wear this dress to marry Phoenix and it's a wedding gift. If you don't, you owe me big time."

"Haley..." She reached out and touched the luxurious lace. This was a dress a princess would wear in a fairy tale.

Or a wedding.

"ARE YOU READY to pack it in?" Paxton asked, sitting next to Phoenix and staring at his phone.

"Just call Lisa and get it over with." His brother was torn about calling his ex.

"It's tempting, but..." He slipped his phone into his pocket. "Let's leave Lisa and Rosie in our past and join Cole and the others and celebrate your victory."

"I'm waiting for Rosie."

"Phoenix..."

He reached for his phone. He'd been resisting calling her. He had to let her make this decision on her own. He didn't want to pressure her. But as hard as it was to admit, it really was her decision. She either loved him enough or she didn't. He'd wait just a little longer.

Jake crawled onto his lap and rested his head on Phoenix's shoulder. His son was tired. He should take him back to the hotel, but something in Phoenix just wouldn't give up.

The door opened and Phoenix turned to see his whole family trail back in. Justin was asleep in his carrier and John was also asleep on Falcon's shoulder. His brothers, Mom and Grandpa were here to support him. His chest swelled with renewed hope.

His mother squeezed in between him and Paxton. "We decided none of us would get any sleep thinking about you here waiting." She touched his arm. "I love you, son, and I want you to be happy. I..."

The door opened again and Phoenix jumped to his feet. It could only be one person. He stared at the woman standing at the back of the church. *Rosie*. He was sure, but it had taken a moment to recognize her in the white lace dress...with feathers. She was beautiful and he couldn't tear his eyes away. She stood there, her blue eyes sparkling, holding Dixie.

He quickly handed a sleepy Jake to Phoenix. "Daddy," Jake muttered.

"Stay with Uncle Pax."

Phoenix turned and saw his mother walking down the aisle to Rosie. No. No. No! But he slowed in his stride to Rosie. His mother had to say what she wanted to.

"You look lovely, dear," his mom said. "You have hair just like your mother's."

Rosie self-consciously touched her hair. "Yes. I take after my mother."

"I always liked Sarah."

"Me, too," Rosie said with a slight grin.

"I have to be honest, dear. I have so many conflicting emotions about this marriage. But you were right when you said a good mother loves and supports her children even when it hurts. This hurts, but I'm going to accept this marriage because I love my son and I don't want to lose him."

"I love him, too."

"Then let's get this wedding started." She looked at the dog in Rosie's arms. "Are you bringing the dog to the wedding?

"Yes, ma'am. Dixie is my family and I couldn't get married without her."

His mother patted Rosie's hands clutched around Dixie. "I think you and I are going to get along just fine. Everyone calls me Miss Kate, but you can call me Kate or whatever you feel comfortable with."

"Thank you, Miss… Kate."

Phoenix released a breath of pure relief. He hugged his mother. "Thank you, Mom."

Then he gathered a smiling Rosie into his arms and kissed her and kissed her until there were just two of them in this church starting a life together. It was magical. It was special. It was family.

Dixie yelped and Jake squeezed in between them. The smiles just grew wider.

"I love you," she whispered.

"I love you, too." He took her hand and led her to the altar, where the minister was waiting. The minister had come in earlier, wanting to close up the church, and Phoenix had begged for a few more minutes. There with his family surrounding him, he married Rosemary McCray, and they vowed to love each other forever. There would be stumbles along the way, but they both were stronger now and were prepared to face whatever they had to.

Together.

# *Epilogue*

*Two weeks later*

The days after their wedding were crazy and busy. They stayed in Rosie's trailer but soon found it was too small for the three of them. Phoenix told his mother he would like the land next to Egan's, and she agreed he could build his home there. His plan was that after riding the rodeo circuit, he and Paxton would start a rodeo contracting business. The land at the end of Rebel Road was perfect for what he had in mind. But they needed a place to live in the meantime.

Egan had a trailer that he and Rachel had lived in while they'd renovated their home. Quincy and Jenny had lived in it while they'd built theirs. It was still hooked up to water and electricity, and Egan suggested that they use it. There was one problem, though—it had only one bedroom. With his brothers' help, Phoenix took the sofa out and put Jake's bed in the spot. The trailer had more room than the one they were living in, and it would do until their home was built.

Even though their life was crazy, they'd adjusted well to the mayhem. Phoenix, Paxton, Rico and Elias had cleared out some land for Phoenix's house. They were looking at house plans, and just as soon as the weather got warmer they would start building.

The cold December wind blew, but the Phoenix Rebel family hardly noticed as they picked up tree limbs to throw on a fire they had going in what would be their yard. Jake ran around picking up twigs and throwing them on the fire. They were going to roast hot dogs and s'mores and sit out and enjoy the evening. But the temperature kept dropping, and Phoenix didn't know how much longer they could stay out. Jake's nose was already red.

Phoenix wrapped his arms around Rosie. "What do you think? Is this a perfect spot for a house or not?"

She leaned back against him. "It's perfect. Grandpa said it was and, you know, I believe everything Grandpa says."

He liked that she called his grandfather Grandpa. That came easy, but calling his mother Kate was a little harder. Rosie had adjusted, though. She'd adjusted to so much, and every day got a little easier.

"Our bedroom and bath are going to look out at the barn and the corral so we can keep an eye on Lady and the horses."

"You got it." He kissed her cold cheek.

"I'm so happy," she murmured. "I never dreamed I could be this happy."

"We've been tested, as they say, and we passed with flying colors."

Jake squeezed between them. He had on his coat and his hood over his head. All they could see was his little face and red nose.

Rosie picked him up. "Are you cold?"

He shook his head. "Cocoa."

"Okay." Rosie carried him to the blanket and their ice

chest by the fire. She poured hot chocolate out of a thermos into his sippy cup. Jake sat down to drink it. Dixie curled up at his feet.

A truck drove through the gate, and Phoenix looked up to see his mother.

"We've got company."

His mother walked toward them. "I saw the smoke and thought I'd check to see what you're up to."

"Just burning some of the debris from the bulldozing," he said.

"It's a lovely spot for a house with all these tall oaks."

Jake ran to his grandmother and held up his arms. She picked him up. "He's doing this more often, and it really makes me happy." She kissed his face. "Do you want to come home with Grandma?"

Jake shook his head. "No, me helping Daddy." Jake was now putting more than one word together and speaking in almost complete sentences. It had seemed to happen overnight.

She set him on his feet and he ran back to the fire, Dixie on his heels.

"Jude, Paige and Zane are out for the evening, and I was hoping I could talk y'all into coming for supper."

His mom was obviously feeling a little lonely. Phoenix glanced at Rosie, and she nodded. "Why don't you join us? We're having hot dogs and s'mores."

"Oh, no. I don't want to intrude."

Rosie took her arm and led her to the blankets they had laid out on the ground. "You're not intruding. We'd love to have you. That is, if you don't mind sitting on a blanket."

His mom sank down by Rosie, and Phoenix watched as the two women got food out of the cooler for hot dogs.

They were getting along better than he'd ever expected. The fire crackled and hissed, keeping them warm. Later they made s'mores, and he laughed as his mother got chocolate on her face. It was a good bonding time.

It began to sprinkle, and they quickly gathered their things to head home. Suddenly his mother hugged Rosie. "I'm sorry for being so bullheaded when Phoenix told me he wanted to marry you. You love each other. I can clearly see that, and I wish nothing but happiness for both of you."

"Thank you, Miss Kate. That means more than you'll ever know."

His mother hugged him and said, "I kind of miss the teasing jokester, but I'm real proud of the strong, dependable, mature young man you've become. Your father would be, too."

He hugged her back. "Thank you, Mom."

The rain picked up and they ran for their trucks. It didn't take them long to get to their trailer. Rosie dashed inside with Jake and he carried Dixie. The trailer had central air and heat, and the warmth felt nice as they stripped out of their coats. Jake was half-asleep, and Rosie quickly undressed him and put him in his bed. She read him a story, but he was out before she even reached the ending.

Phoenix sat in a recliner, and Rosie curled onto his lap. "I had a good time with your mother tonight. She is nice, just like everyone said she was."

He kissed her neck. "See, you worried for nothing."

"Did I tell you today how much I love you?"

He tucked a strand of hair behind her ear. "This morning, but you can tell me again in about five minutes. I've got the tub full of hot bubbly water, and you and I are going to take a long, long bath."

She rested her face against his. "I'm finally home. Really home."

"No more doubts?"

"Not a one."

"I'll love you forever," he whispered against her lips, and that was a promise he intended to keep, no matter what happened in their lives.

Forever was all the time they needed.

\* \* \* \* \*

*There are two Rebel men who are still single!*
*Watch for the next story*
*in Linda Warren's* TEXAS REBELS *miniseries,*
*TEXAS REBELS: PAXTON,*
*coming December 2016,*
*only from Harlequin Western Romance!*

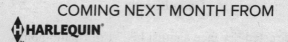

SPECIAL EXCERPT FROM

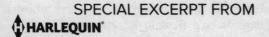
HARLEQUIN®

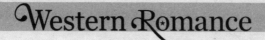
Western Romance

*The minute he recovers from injury, Trace Delaney
will get back to bull riding, pick up and move on as
he always does. But can Annie Owen and her twin
daughters change his mind?*

*Read on for a sneak preview of
THE BULL RIDER'S HOMECOMING,
the second book in Jeannie Watt's
MONTANA BULL RIDERS miniseries.*

The girls were waiting at the top of the stairs when Annie
opened the cellar door. They high-fived their mom, and
Trace grinned as they went to stand on the heater vents
when the furnace began to blow.

"No more dollar eating," Katie announced.

"Just the normal amount of dollar eating," Annie
corrected before shooting a look Trace's way.

Dismissed?

"Well…those chores are waiting," he said.

"We can play a game next time you come by," Kristen
assured him.

Trace crouched down in front of her, feeling only a little
awkward as he said, "I look forward to that. And it was a
lot of fun riding with you guys today."

"We're not guys. We're girls," Kristen informed him.

"I stand corrected," Trace said as he got to his feet.
Tough crowd.

"I'll walk you to your truck," Annie said.

Escorted from the premises. So much for that whisper of disappointment he'd thought he saw cross her face. Maybe he was the one who was disappointed. But he'd promised to leave as soon as the furnace was fixed, and he was a man of his word.

Annie slipped into her coat and followed Trace out of the house. The air was still brisk from the storm, but the setting sun cast warm golden light over Annie's neatly kept yard. Everything about her place was warm and homey, the exact opposite of what he knew when he'd been growing up. He hoped the twins would look back in the years ahead and appreciate the home their mother had made for them.

Trace stopped before opening his truck door and looked down at Annie, who was wearing a cool expression. The woman was hard to read. On the one hand, he thought maybe she liked him. On the other, she couldn't hurry him out of there fast enough.

"Thanks again," she said.

"Anytime." One corner of his mouth quirked up before he said, "I mean that, you know."

Annie's lips compressed and she nodded, then she raised her hand and brushed her fingers against his cheek just as he'd done to her earlier. He felt his breath catch at the light touch. Then he captured her hand with his and leaned down to take her lips in a kiss that surprised both of them.

*Don't miss*
*THE BULL RIDER'S HOMECOMING*
*by Jeannie Watt, available September 2016 wherever*
*Harlequin® Western Romance*
*books and ebooks are sold.*

www.Harlequin.com

# *Wrangle Your Friends for the Ultimate Ranch Girls' Getaway*

**Win an all-expenses-paid 3-night luxurious stay for you and your 3 guests at The Resort at Paws Up in Greenough, Montana.**

## Retail Value $10,000

### A TOAST TO FRIENDSHIP, AN ADVENTURE OF A LIFETIME!

Learn more at
www.Harlequinranchgetaway.com

## Sweepstakes ends August 31, 2016

WCHMR

HARLEQUIN®
A *Romance* FOR EVERY MOOD™

# Love the Harlequin book you just read?

Your opinion matters.

Review this book on your favorite
book site, review site, blog or your own
social media properties and share
your opinion with other readers!

Be sure to connect with us at:
Harlequin.com/Newsletters
Facebook.com/HarlequinBooks
Twitter.com/HarlequinBooks

**H HARLEQUIN®**

A *Romance* FOR EVERY MOOD™

# JUST CAN'T GET ENOUGH?

Join our social communities
and talk to us online.

You will have access to the latest
news on upcoming titles and special
promotions, but most importantly,
you can talk to other fans about your
favorite Harlequin reads.

Harlequin.com/Community

f Facebook.com/HarlequinBooks

🐦 Twitter.com/HarlequinBooks

P Pinterest.com/HarlequinBooks

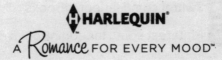